THE CONNELLY CRIME FAMILY BOOK ONE

FOUR NIGHTS

Forever

KB WINTERS

Copyright and Disclaimer

This book is a work of fiction. The names, characters, places and incidents are products of the writer's imagination and have been used fictitiously and are not to be construed as real. Any resemblance to persons, living or dead, actual events, locales or organizations is entirely coincidental.

Table of Contents

Four Nights Forever

The Connelly Crime Family Book 1

By Wall Street Journal & USA Today Bestselling Author KB Winters

Chapter One

Layla

"Hey Layla, you did a great job today. Thanks for stepping in with that idea."

Ross was the Marketing Director and had just promoted me to project manager for the biggest ad agency in Rocket, Nevada. At the awesomely young age of twenty-five, thank you very much.

"I can't believe how off base I was about that pitch," he added.

Ross was a really good boss. He encouraged me to step up more, to speak up instead of letting the senior people on the team, those with the loudest voices get all the glory. But he was an older man in a young, good-looking body.

"I read about it in the comment section of some news site," I said, "and I thought it was a troll or a prank until I did a little digging and found out that yeah, fidget spinners are a thing."

Apparently, kids did crazy things all the time, the only difference was that the older I got, the crazier it all seemed.

"Fidget spinners," he grumbled, looking a little bewildered at how close the firm had come to not landing that huge sneaker account. "I thought those were toys for animals."

"Well," I said, a laugh exploding out of me at the disbelief in Ross's voice. "We don't have to enjoy playing with them. We just have to dangle a free fidget spinner in front of customers to get them to buy these sneakers."

"I suppose you're right," he said, tossing the sample aside on his desk. "What are you up to tonight? Mary bought out a shoe store and she's eager for your input."

I loved his soon-to-be fiancée, that was if he ever got off his ass and put that ring he bought five months ago on her finger, but I had plans tonight. "No can do tonight. I need to check on my dad." My dad, the perpetual mess of a man, whom I loved dearly.

A look of sympathy flashed on Ross's tanned face, pity flickering in his deep brown eyes. "How is your dad, Layla?"

I shrugged. That was about as accurate as I could be when it came to Dad. "He's still breathing, and I make sure he eats enough not to pass out, so ... good?"

Ross nodded slowly. He just didn't get it, and honestly, I didn't expect him to. Most people probably would have washed their hands of my dad years ago when he first fell apart, but I couldn't. Something happened to him while I was in California at college. I didn't know what, but it had changed him. And not for the better.

"Okay, girl. If you need anything, don't hesitate to call us."

"Thanks, Ross. Go home and let Mary model those new shoes for you." With a wiggle of my eyebrows

I left my boss laughing in his office and packed my shit up so I could go home.

As soon as I was in my car, I pulled up my favorite image of Dad on my phone. Mid-laugh with that network of little lines around his eyes and mouth that I loved. He was laughing so hard, he had squinched his blue eyes closed and the sun glinted off his thick, wavy blond hair. He was young, then. Vibrant. Happy. I tapped the image and the sound of the phone ringing came in through the Bluetooth speakers. "Hey Dad, you okay?"

"Yeah, princess, I'm good." By good, he probably meant drunk, since that was his natural state lately. Some days I wondered why I was so eager to graduate from UCLA and come back to Rocket for this shit. A father who was drunk more often than sober, stressed and in need of a weeklong nap.

"How are you?" He slurred the question, but it seemed sincere enough.

"I'm fine, Dad. Just leaving the office. Have you eaten anything today?"

"What time is it?" The next sound was of him digging around his nightstand, probably for his watch, because he was old school like that. If there was any doubt of his sobriety level, it was demolished by the sound of him knocking everything off the nightstand.

Or maybe he'd fallen asleep in his recliner and I was hearing beer cans and bottles falling off the little pine end table that hadn't moved from the spot since I was eight years old. "Oh, no I haven't eaten yet, princess. I'll find something."

"Yeah? What are you going to eat? When was the last time you even went to the grocery store?"

"Last week, maybe. Don't worry about it, your old man will be fine."

Yeah, if I let him he'd 'fine' his way right into an early grave. "Well I *am* worried about it, Dad. I need to stop at the store anyway so I'll bring you some things. Why don't you take a shower and clean up before I get there and we can have dinner together?"

Dad cleared his throat, coughed and cleared his throat once again. I called it the wakeup call of the chain smoking drunk. "Sure, princess, that sounds good. See you soon." I hated how things had deteriorated between us ever since I'd become the adult in the relationship.

I wanted to tell him about boys I dated, which lately had been exactly zero, and talk about stupid work problems and gossip about some chick who was prettier than me. But we couldn't. Every conversation was me nagging him to eat, to shower, to take care of himself. To pay his bills. And then it was Dad reminding me that he was an adult, capable of taking care of himself. It was antagonistic at best and the scoff he let out before hanging up hurt like hell.

But this was my new reality. This was the dream I went to college to fulfill. It seemed like I might have been better off staying in Rocket and making it work with community college and in-state tuition. Every other goddamn hour it felt like I was regretting taking that scholarship and leaving Nevada, but I had to. I needed to, dammit.

The problems with Dad had started while I was in California and the guilt ate at me every time I looked into his deep blue eyes and saw a shadow of the man who'd raised me. It ate at me then and it ate at me now. Practically killed me to see him like that.

I grabbed a cart and made my way through the supermarket to do shopping for two. I guessed that was less pathetic than shopping for one, but with Dad to take care of, I didn't have the energy or patience to take care of another man.

Though I wouldn't mind having someone to take care of my own needs. For a little while, anyway.

Chapter Two

Eamon

"I told her I'd give her a grand for every second she kept me in her mouth." My little brother Shae was a goddamn riot.

"How long did you hold her down there?" Shea was a damn freak and had almost a fetish-like love for getting head.

Shae frowned but his satisfaction over whatever he was about to say was too great and he flashed a wide, shit eating grin. "I didn't have to do shit but lie back and enjoy it while Sonya tried to kill herself for a few dollars."

"A few?"

He shrugged, still grinning from ear to ear. "I may have fucked her mouth a little and didn't last as long as I wanted."

"How long?"

"Thirty grand, that's how long." The sick fuck was actually embarrassed by that.

"Expensive blow job."

"That's where you're wrong, E-money. The blow job was for her, to lube her up for the party later. By the time I gave her orgasm number two she was begging me to take her ass." He licked his lips and adjusted his pants at the memory.

"You have issues, baby brother."

He shrugged and took a swig of the icy vodka he kept on tap whenever we came to our father's place for business. "Just enough to make me irresistible to the wrong kind of women."

That much was true. Whatever scars the Connelly men had in our past, we all dealt with them in our own way.

At twenty-four, Shae was just six years younger than me, but people could tell we were brothers. We both had our mother's fair skin and the same frame, lean, ripped and always ready for battle. And we both had dimples, though his was on his cheek and mine was on my chin. Back in elementary school, the kids teased us about them, but we'd always had the last laugh because the Connelly dimples were chick magnets.

Shae fucked his demons away. I did too sometimes, but my preferred method of purging was fighting. Pounding. Obliterating. Which was why I'd been the designated enforcer for years.

"Where's Rourke?" I asked Shae after he finished gloating about his latest score.

"In the study with the old man." Rourke was the most serious of all three of us, probably had something to do with losing his dad at a young age and growing up in this life with his mom, my Aunt Fiona. "They're talking about the books."

The books. How the Connelly family made our money. Gambling and betting were our main trade but as a criminal organization we dabbled in everything from drugs to guns and made millions a year dealing in ass. We sold ass. All ages, colors, and kinks. All told, we ran the city of Rocket, Nevada, nestled in the Truckee

Valley, which kept the family coffers overflowing and it was our job as the next generation to keep it that way. "Anything wrong?" I asked, looking over my brother's shoulder.

"Just basic accounting," Shae answered, which was code for *The List*. The names of debts that had been left hanging too long without payment. Which meant it was time for me to make a few visits and maybe, hopefully, break a few bones. I grinned at the thought.

Before I could say anything else, Rourke joined us in the game room, slipping the pool stick from my hands. "Uncle Patrick wants to see you, Eamon."

It probably made me the same sick fuck I accused Shae of being for feeling a thrill as I took the steps that led me to my father's study. It was just what you'd expect of a very rich man who was too fucking concerned with appearances. Dark, mahogany wood made up nearly the whole damn room from the large intimidating desk, the wet bar in the corner, the tables scattered around the room and even the floor to ceiling bookshelves on the wall to the left. What wasn't dark wood was black or brown leather. "You wanted to see me?"

He nodded, his sharp green eyes hadn't dulled a bit despite his age, though at fifty-five, Patrick Connelly was one of the younger mob bosses in the area. His brown hair was more silver these days which only made his eyes even more intense. "I did. Come in, son. I have a special task for you."

There went those tingles again, like the first spark of a fire dancing on my skin at the thought of working out some of my demons. "Whatever you need, Father."

Patrick nodded, pleased with the answer even though we both knew there was no other acceptable answer. "Peter Michaels. His payments have stopped and the local muscle hasn't done a good job of impressing upon him the importance of paying me my fucking money. I need you to show him how unwise that is."

Shit. Peter Michaels was a sad sack of a man who gave me no pleasure to threaten or beat. I'd do it because it was my job, because it was part of the family business, but goddammit I wouldn't enjoy it. He was weak. Pathetic. "No problem, Dad. I'm on it. Anything else?"

I knew the deal, but I let my father explain it every damn time because it was something he apparently needed to do.

"Michaels isn't some rich fuck who just doesn't want to pay his debt, so remind him just enough that he'll remember the lesson *while* he works his nine to five."

"Got it," I said.

Without another word, I left the study and made my way through the green and white spiral tile that marked the path to the front door. I hopped in my blue Benz and made my way to the slightly rundown area of Rocket where Peter Michaels lived. Thankfully, alone.

The gray cement buildings were all the same, with the same green painted metal railing fixed to the cement and steel staircases. The side of each building held a numbered stencil and I found a spot right in front of number three. Taking the stairs three at a time, I found unit 310 and knocked, stepping just out of view of the peephole in case Michaels had any thoughts of running or playing possum.

"Hey ... Mr. Connelly," his smile died on his lips. "W-what are you doing here?"

"We both know exactly what I'm doing here," I told him as I pushed inside and removed my jacket. "Come into any money recently?" I was happy I'd decided to go with a shirt with buttons so I wouldn't have to remove cufflinks to roll up my sleeves.

"Uh, no. I haven't. And I don't have any money for you today."

Of course he didn't because that would make my job, my life too fucking simple and if there was one thing my life never was? Easy.

"But I'll get it, I promise."

That old story. I wasn't falling for it. "Sorry. Out of time. You know what has to be done." I cracked my knuckles, not to scare him, just because it was something I did.

Michaels nodded, resigned to his fate the way gambling addicts always were. "I know but ... I just ... can you give me more time? I just need more time."

"That is the one thing you don't have, Peter." I grabbed him by the collar and sent my fist smashing down on his face. Once. Twice. Three hits right to the nose. The mouth. The jaw. "Now, do you have an answer for me?"

"No! No," he gasped, trying to catch his breath. "I don't have any money for you, but I will. Soon. I promise."

I punched him again because the promises of a gambling addict meant less than shit to me. "Wrong answer, Michaels. Wanna try again?"

Blood streamed from his nose, his brow and the corner of his mouth and still I didn't feel any sense of relief. That frustration forced me to land another series of blows right to his pudgy gut.

"Okay, okay!" he pleaded.

I released the pathetic excuse for a man and he took a step back, swiping blood from the corner of his mouth, spitting some on the floor. "How long can you give me?"

"End of the week. No more." He nodded excitedly, grateful even and I knew I hadn't gotten my point across. "I'm not fucking around with you, Michaels."

"Of course not. End of the week is perfect, by then I'll be able to ... ow! What the hell was that for?"

I got in his face, close enough that I could see how fear transformed his eyes into a light, sea color. "That was to remind you that if the end of the week rolls around and you don't have what you owe, *to put you current,* you'll be wishing for what I did to you tonight." I landed one more for good measure when I heard the twist of the knob.

A shrill scream. "Stop! Fucker! Stop hitting him you fucking asshole! That's my dad!"

I stopped and turned to look at the screamer over my shoulder. Damn, she was hot. Stacked and curvy as fuck. Blonde, just how I liked 'em and with a mouth that only a filthy motherfucker like me could tame. She wore some kind of sexy office girl outfit, a tight skirt that showed off a slim waist, big tits and hips that were more than a handful. But it was those thick, fuck-me red lips that drew my attention and made my cock wake up and take notice. "Someone should tell your *dad* the importance of paying his fucking debts."

"Debts?" She looked shocked, confused, which I was more than prepared for.

Why?

Because family was always the last to know.

Chapter Three

Layla

My heart raced about a million miles an hour as that tall, gorgeous man with the gold and green eyes glared at me, talking nonsense about debts. "Maybe you ought to get your facts straight, asshole. My dad doesn't have any debts. I made sure of it."

When I came home from college a few years ago, I noticed that my father couldn't survive without a little adult supervision. I took over paying his bills after coming over to find the electricity and water had been shut off and the phone didn't work.

Gorgeous Asshole, which is how I now thought of him, didn't seem at all put off by my statement. In fact, the fucker smirked. It was the move arrogant jerks all over the world used. Only with this particular jerk, there was a dimple on his cheek that made him even more devastatingly handsome. And I was a sick daughter to even think of him like that.

"Is that right?" he said.

I nodded, confident in my words because I knew the bills were paid, but still the "Yep," I squeaked out sounded less sure. I blamed it on his proximity and the fact that he'd bloodied my dad's face.

He turned to Dad. "You mean to tell me this pretty little thing has been taking care of your bills and you didn't tell her about the most important one?"

Gorgeous Asshole shook his head and smacked his lips as he pulled back his fist and let it go, smack in the center of Dad's face.

"Stop it!" The bags of groceries finally fell from my arms, hitting the floor with an unimpressive thud thanks to my five-foot-three frame. "Stop hitting him!" I ran the few feet to reach him, stepping between his raised fist and my battered father. "Just fucking stop, will you? We'll get this figured out. Just stop!"

I looked up at him and again, I was struck by how good-looking he was. Too good looking to be a guy who beat people up for a living.

"It's okay, princess," my dad croaked out.

I turned to my dad, frowning so hard I felt a headache coming on, or maybe it was this fucked up situation triggering a migraine. "What do you mean it's okay? It's not fucking okay, Dad, to let this guy beat you up over money." After helping him into his favorite recliner, I turned to Gorgeous Asshole and aimed a candy apple red nail at him. "You! I should call the cops on you, coming in here to beat up on an old, unsuspecting drunk. What is your problem?"

His lips, thick and full, formed into a perfect pout, twitched in amusement, which only pissed me off more. I was tired of people, specifically men, underestimating me. They either looked at me like a sex object or an incapable little girl. And I wasn't either one.

"My problem is that your father owes the family money and he hasn't paid. In weeks."

A shiver slid down my spine at the deep timber of his voice, that scratchy, guttural sound that hit all the right nerve endings. "And so you thought beating the crap out of him would get your money faster? What in the hell kind of business is *the family* running?" I put up my fingers in air quotes. The Family. Hah!

"The polite reminders don't seem to be working."

Polite? "Polite? What a fucking joke! Polite? Let's see how polite you are when the boys in blue show up." Confident that would end this whole mess without Dad needing a trip to the ER, I reached for my phone and swiped to unlock the screen.

"I wouldn't do that if I were you." His voice changed. It was still low but the seductive quality now sounded lethal. Deadly.

"Oh yeah, and why not? Oh that's right, because *you* don't want to go to jail. Well guess what, buddy? I don't want my—" The words died on my lips when I looked up at the unfamiliar clicking sound that sounded close.

Too close.

"If you involve the police, this will get messy and I promise you, *princess*," he said the word derogatively and my hands balled into fists, "you don't want this kind of messy."

I didn't even know what the hell that meant but I believed that he knew of a type of messy I couldn't possibly dream up and wanted no part of. My gaze went to the gun he held in his hand. His steady, non-shaking hand showed he was comfortable with a gun. Too comfortable. "Fine, I won't call. Yet," I clarified. He might have the gun, but that didn't mean Gorgeous Asshole would win. If he killed us, he would never get his money. That thought didn't stop the knot in my gut though. "How much is this debt, Dad?"

He looked up at me. One eye was swollen shut. His lip was split, and he had blood and bruises all over his face. My heart sank. He was so messed up. "Don't worry about it, honey. I'm grown. I'll handle this."

"Wrong answer. You're the dad, but *I'm* the grownup here and I can't possibly attempt to help you if I don't know how much you owe." He dipped his head low in embarrassment but his mouth remained shut and I turned to the green-eyed pummeler. "Well?"

Gorgeous Asshole replied, "It's more money than you have, *princess*. It's a lot and it needs to be paid. Now."

Why did this man try to make everything he said sound like an invitation to get naked and sweaty? "Well how the hell am I supposed to pay it if you won't tell me the amount, genius?"

"Layla, stop. Please. Eamon don't hurt her."

So Eamon was his name. Go figure with that smooth, shiny brown hair and those colorful eyes that I bet were sixteen shades of trouble. "I won't stop, Dad. You owe him money, how much?" Both men nodded. "Great, so somebody tell me how much and I'll get it paid."

Now neither of them had anything to say. No surprise there. "I'm handling it, Layla."

"Yeah *Layla*, he's handling it," the annoying Eamon said.

"Just because this dick gets off on beating the shit out of people doesn't make it handled. How did this happen, Dad? What is the money for?"

"Oh, fuck," Eamon grumbled behind me, a sound that was equal parts disbelief and worry.

"Just a run of bad luck at the tables."

"The tables? What tables?" His clear eye, the one that wasn't already swollen shut, gave me a look that said I couldn't possibly be that stupid and now, it all made sense. He owed money not to Eamon's family, but to *The Family*. Rocket may not have been Las Vegas, but I knew exactly what family with a capital 'F' meant.

Bloody reminders.

Cement shoes.

Bodies in the desert.

Debts paid one way or another.

"You borrowed money from the Connelly mob to fucking *gamble*? Dad, how could you?" I was beyond disappointed, beyond disgusted and deep down, terrified for my dad. Though it occurred to me that maybe I should be worried about me as well, now that I knew who and what, Eamon was.

"I figured the streak had to heat up again, princess. Remember that year we went to Disney? That was a good year."

"Disney? Dad, I was twelve when that happened." Mom had been dead for four years already and Dad had been a shell of himself, but still mostly happy and not quite as stressed. "Wait, you've been gambling since then? How in the hell did I not know this?"

He nodded, not at all ashamed which pissed me off even more. "Your mom helped me keep things under control but without her, I'm useless. I'm sorry, honey."

Shit. I couldn't take this anymore. I turned back to Eamon. "What can we do to settle this gambling debt?"

Chapter Four

Eamon

She was feisty. I liked a feisty woman, they kept my dick hard all night long and if I let them, well into the morning. I knew what desire looked like and sweet, sassy Layla wanted me. I saw the way her big blue eyes landed on the muscles of my forearms, the way they went wide and her breath hitched. She hated my guts, I could see that too.

But she also wanted me. And that fucking turned me on more than anything.

"I'm just going to get my dad cleaned up," she said, every syllable dripping with disdain. "Unless of course you want to beat on him some more?" Her eyes narrowed in anger as she stared up at me but all I could focus on was her mouth. Lush red lips and they weren't painted on, nope, they were the burnished kind that looked more natural. The color that stayed long after she'd make me come with those perfect lips. The perfect dick-sucking mouth.

"Nah, I don't think you need any further reminders, do you Petey?" He shook his head and grinned at her. "Then go ahead and get the old man cleaned up. I'll be right here."

"No need. You can go."

I laughed this time because this girl had energy. She should be scared. Hell, she should be fucking terrified of me, but she wasn't. And it was hot as fuck. "I think I'll wait right here."

She glared at me so hard, I could barely see the blue in her eyes before she dismissed me and helped her father down the hall.

I didn't mind. It gave me time to think about something I had no business thinking about, but with her spicy floral perfume still swirling in the air, it was the only damn thing I *could* think about. Layla. Even her name and the sight of those curves brought to mind that old song. Smooth rhythms, hot sex and late nights. I wanted Layla, that much was certain.

The only uncertain thing was what in the hell was I prepared to do about it.

How in the hell did a pathetic sack of shit like Peter Michaels produce that spitfire of a woman? She was bubbly and she was brave, standing up to me the way she did and in defense of a man who damn sure didn't deserve it. A confident woman was sexy. But a woman with a good reason to be confident *and* could back it up? Well, that was a woman who belonged in my bed. Under me. On top of me.

Coming around my cock.

Damn, I needed to stop thinking with my dick and start thinking with my brain. There was no way in hell I could lead the family into the future if I let my cock guide me when it came to business decisions. That was Shae's downfall. Then again, this might be exactly the kind of lesson our debtors needed to learn.

"Is there a reason you're still here?" Layla returned from the bathroom alone, which was probably for the best.

"You wanted to know if there was some other way to repay your father's debt."

"Yeah." Arms crossed defensively, tapping her foot, she looked like she was ready to bolt or kick me in the nuts. Too bad I'd put my piece away already. Not that I'd use it on her, but fear was a sweet aphrodisiac. "And?"

"I've decided there is a way. Would you like to hear it?" I was stalling because I needed a few more moments to think things through, to make sure this was worth the risk I'd be taking. If I did this, the money would have to come from someplace.

"Well don't keep me in suspense here."

Her attitude, even in the face of massive debt, decided for me. "I want you. In my bed. A hot night of fucking at my place. Me and you."

She laughed. Tossed her blonde hair back and laughed with her whole body. If I wasn't having such a good time watching her tits—all natural—jiggle as she did it, I might have been upset. "You want me to date you—"

"No, not date. Fuck. You know, now that I think about it, daddy's debt is kind of a big deal. Let's make it four nights. All night until morning or until I ask you to leave. When the fourth night is over, your father's debt will be free and clear."

Layla opened her mouth to argue, probably to berate me, but I could tell the moment she got it. Really got it. She wanted me, so fucking me, letting me have my way with her body would be no hardship for her. I would make sure she was satisfied, and she'd come out a winner twice—no four times. "Four nights? You can't be serious."

"I am serious, Layla. I never joke about money—or fucking." I had what I wanted for the moment. My words would linger in her mind for the rest of the night. She wouldn't be able to think about anything but me.

My offer. What it might be like to fuck me. "I'll find you tomorrow when I'll expect an answer or the debt payment, your choice."

"Right. Until then, I guess." She sounded put out and slightly beaten but the little hellcat wasn't out of the fight. Not yet.

"Try not to get into any trouble between now and then." There was a little too much glee in her voice and that only made me laugh again.

"And miss out on four nights of fucking? I wouldn't dream of it. *princess.*" I left the apartment and closed the door just as a can came sailing at my head.

Yeah, this would be fun.

Chapter Five

Layla

I was still fuming over Eamon's so-called proposition as I moved around Dad's kitchen, whipping up a casserole for him to eat over the next few days. Making far more noise than cheeseburger noodle casserole required, my thoughts and my anger were all twisted up and aimed at Eamon. And Dad. If not for these two fucked up men—both awful in their own ways—I could be at home relaxing in the bath with a tall glass of Jack & Coke. Instead, I was chopping onions and green peppers to add to the ground beef, grating cheese and being domestic.

Fuck, these guys pissed me off!

Why in the hell was I doing *this* when the man sitting in his faithful fucking recliner was the one who'd had all the fun from spending all the money he'd borrowed? Why was I forced to step up and do the unthinkable just to keep him out of trouble? The more questions flashed in my mind, the angrier I got and the more noise I made in the kitchen. I knew what I had to do. Hell I'd do just about anything to keep harm from coming to my dad, even though he hadn't thought about the future, about how he'd pay the money back. Or what would happen if he didn't.

"Layla, please."

Please? Was he seriously giving me shit about the noise I made while I cooked meals *for him*? "Please what, Dad?" I turned to stare angry daggers at him through the wall but there he stood, right in the doorway staring at me with sad blue eyes, well one sad blue eye and one swollen shut purple eye.

"Please don't do whatever it is Eamon Connelly asked you to do in order to forgive my debt." He looked so broken and not just physically. Dad used to be a vibrant man so full of life that he was like a magnet, pulling everyone around him into his orbit. When Mom was alive, they'd been so happy and so in love, I envied that. Wanted it for myself someday because it made me believe in true love.

But if I thought watching her die had been hard, watching him slowly die every damn day since was killing me. It had taught me a valuable lesson about love. It was a trap. Sure, you might end up like those couples who were happy together for fifty or sixty years. That would be amazing and beautiful. But for most people, you found that the sick, cruel universe conspired to take love from you.

By any means necessary.

The sorrow and the cruelty were written all over my dad's face, tearing me apart one tethered shred at a time. "What makes you think he asked me to do anything?"

He sighed and raked a shaky hand through his damp hair, no longer greasy and stringy since his quick shower. "Because I know Eamon and more importantly, I know how the Connelly family operates."

I scoffed out loud at the certainty in his voice. "Oh, do you? Is that why you borrowed a sum so big neither of you cowards will tell me? Or worse, why you refused to pay them back, because you know them so well?" He opened his mouth to offer some excuse, but I was tired of them. "Because if you knew them so well, were you so damn worried about what they might do that you might have, I don't know, paid them back? Or at least had the decency to tell me I might walk in and find some gangster beating the ever-loving crap out of you!"

"Princess, please—"

"No Dad, don't princess me. I'm not in the mood for it. You know what happens if you don't have that money by the end of the week, right?"

His shoulders drooped and his head fell forward, giving me a quick glance at the thinning top of his graying blond hair. "Yeah, I know. And it's my problem, not yours."

Could this insane person really be my father? "Tell me you're kidding. Please tell me that you don't think them maiming or killing you is somehow *not* my problem!" I sounded hysterical and I knew it, but the thing was, this version of my dad was infuriating.

This wasn't the same man who'd come to my volleyball games and cheered so loud he annoyed the other parents and the coaches. It wasn't the same man who'd cheer loudly during my debate club performances, who'd taught me to ride a bike and who let me eat mashed potatoes and ice cream for a week after I broke my arm while attempting to fly out of a tree. No, this guy was a much paler, weaker, beaten down version of that guy. And as much as I loved him, I didn't like him at all.

But I knew my dad was still in there somewhere and I had to believe he was because it was the only way I'd agree to Eamon's degrading plan without hating myself for the rest of my life.

"You can't trust him," he said.

Another laugh escaped and this one was more bitter than the last. "Of course I can't trust him, Dad. I wonder if there's anyone I can trust, but that's not really the point. is it? I know I can't trust you to pay back the money before they kill you, which means I have to trust that man to keep his word."

"And if he doesn't?"

"Well then fuck, at least I know I did my best," I spat out, tired of the bullshit.

It was a question I'd already asked myself and there was no satisfying answer. If I spent four days in Eamon's bed and he still enforced the debt, then selling my body would be the least of my worries. "If he doesn't then you'll likely be dead in the desert and I'll have more important things to worry about. Like other fucking gangsters coming to me to pay off your stupid debts."

"You don't know Eamon," he insisted, worry and fear clouding his eyes.

He was right, I didn't. Other than what I'd heard about him through the Rocket grapevine, which I tried to avoid, I knew very little about Gorgeous Asshole. But I knew he was hot as fuck, and if I'd met him under normal circumstances, I would have wanted to get naked with him, which meant I knew my answer. As if I had a choice in the matter. "No, I don't but I *do* know that if I don't agree with him, then I'll be signing your death warrant."

"Maybe that's what needs to happen. We both know I haven't been the same since your mom passed. Without your mom here, I'm afraid everything has turned to shit. When you left for college, I was glad, happy that you wouldn't see me like this." He motioned to his battered face with a sharp laugh. "But now I've put you right in the center of my shit show, which was the last thing I ever wanted."

"Oh, so now you're suicidal? Why didn't you tell me about your gambling problem? Did Mom know how bad it was?"

He nodded. "She did and she put limits on me. No more than a hundred bucks every now and then because that was all we could afford to lose without suffering, and it worked well."

"Until it didn't."

Dad nodded again. "My grief over losing your mother was bad, sweetheart. Most days I didn't know how to deal with it. How to cope. Once you were in high school and didn't need me to make sure you got up on time or finished your homework, it was an excuse to let go. Let the addiction consume me."

The regret that his face displayed only strengthened my resolve. "I'll do this, Dad, because I have to. I love you and you're all I have left in this world, so whatever I need to do to keep you safe, I'll do it."

"I know, I just wish you didn't have to."

That made two of us because, as much as my body might be screaming out that I was a big fat fucking liar because I wanted Eamon, I was worried that I might hate my dad forever for putting me in this position. And if that was the case, was it even worth it? "Yeah, me too."

But everything about this situation had trouble written all over it and as certainty and resolve settled around my shoulders like one of those super cute sophisticated New York City cloaks, another unwelcome sensation crept in...

Trouble.

Whatever happened during the next four nights, I was sure I wouldn't walk away the same woman I was today.

Chapter Six

Eamon

Hiding out inside of a dark dive bar frequented by mid-level business managers who wanted to make sure their wives and girlfriends never found out about each other was not my idea of a good night. In fact, I was pretty sure it was one of the circles of hell, fueled by cheap cologne, cheaper perfume and half-priced well drinks. But I needed some time to think.

I needed to come up with an explanation for why I didn't have one fucking dollar of the money Peter Michaels owed the family. Staring at my swollen, bloody knuckles, I knew damn well I couldn't tell my father that I couldn't resist the man's daughter and had decided to let him repay the debt with her body. If I did that, he'd laugh with that sharp glint in his eye that had made more than a few hardened gangsters tremble in their boots. Then he would tell me what he always did.

"If she's willing to do that, let's put her to work and get all my money back. With interest."

And even though I didn't know anything about Layla, except that I wanted to fuck her, I didn't want that fate for her. This wasn't her debt, it was her old man's. And what was worse was the surprise written on her face when she realized that she was the only one in the room surprised by the beat down and the debt. She hadn't even known he was a gambler, so no, I wouldn't put her to work in one of the Connelly's whorehouses, strip clubs or escort agencies.

No, Layla was mine. For four long beautiful nights, she would be mine. In my bed, up against the wall, in the shower. However I wanted to take that delectable body with mouthwatering curves, I would.

Hard and fast, slow and intense, wild and out of control. I had four days of total access and I had no qualms about taking them in exchange for the money.

Men loved to pretend they didn't pay for sex but we all did. One way or another, we paid. Married guys paid with mortgages and family vacations; single guys paid with expensive meals the women didn't eat, overpriced cars to reel in the prettiest of the bunch. We all paid in the hoops we jumped through, issuing just the right compliment instead of telling a chick she had great tits or a nice round ass, kissing her chastely on her doorstep and forking over cash for two more dates just so *she* felt comfortable enough to spread her legs.

Yeah, we all paid in some way, shape or form. The only difference was this time, we both knew what was expected going in. There were no games to be played. I wanted her body and to save her dad, Layla would give it to me.

An hour later and I still didn't have a valid excuse to give for the lack of money in my hands. I shook off the cheap whiskey buzz and made my way to my car and headed toward my dad's house.

By the time I walked through the doors of my father's house, I was stone cold sober and ready with a believable excuse for not collecting the debt.

"Well, well, the prodigal son has finally returned." Rourke's dark stare honed in with a little too much focus for my liking. My cousin saw too damn much with those keen eyes. Usually I appreciated it, but right now I just wanted him to go the hell away. "Everything cool?"

That was how Rourke checked in and it was what I loved most about him. He wanted to know all the details but we were men and he accepted what I told him while also being prepared to jump in and help if need be. "Yeah, everything's cool. He won't like what I have to say but it is what it is."

"I'm sure you have your reasons," Rourke said with confidence, swirling the amber liquid in his glass slowly. "Uncle Patrick is in a mood so tread carefully with your news."

I frowned. My father was an intense and ruthless man but usually he enjoyed his work, even the dirty parts. Hell, if you asked me, he enjoyed the *dirtier* parts of running a criminal organization most of all. "Anything in particular?"

"Shae took exception to the way one of the johns left one of our girls and broke his ribs. The asshole was threatening to sue until I reminded him that his pregnant wife might take all of his money if she knew about his little side habit." Rourke grinned, so pleased when he could play Machiavelli instead of just the mob accountant role Patrick had relegated him to.

"Nice. Shae in there?"

"Hell no. Uncle reamed his ass and he took off like a bat out of hell. My guess is he's somewhere half shit-faced with at least two chicks at his side."

I laughed. "Lucky him. I'm going in."

"Good luck," Rourke called out sarcastically. I knew he didn't believe I'd need it. Both my cousin and my brother were certain I was Patrick's favorite but if that was true, it was news to me. I knew he loved his sons and also loved his sister's son as if Rourke were his own, but Patrick didn't play favorites, not in the way they thought. He respected me because of the role I played within the organization. I wasn't the only one who cracked skulls and broke knees when it was necessary. But as the first-born son of the Connelly family, it was a little odd that I had taken to this particular job so well

Because of my role as enforcer, people feared me, and because of my relationship to Patrick, they also respected me. It meant I had the perfect combination to take his place when the time came, but that didn't mean I was his favorite. I was just the most useful.

For now.

I took a deep breath and knocked on his study door.

"Come in."

When I opened the door, Patrick sat behind his desk with his head resting on the back of the chair and his eyes closed.

"Is this a good time?" I asked.

He groaned and pushed away from the desk. A thin young redhead wearing a scrap of white Lycra that was pretending to be a dress knelt at his feet. With obvious disappointment, he said, "Let's pick this up later, Jacinda."

"You got it, Mr. Connelly." She rose to her feet, adjusted the Lycra to cover her essentials and gave a cute little finger wave to Dad without sparing me a glance as she left. Smart girl, knowing who had the real power in the room.

"You got my money?" He didn't even wait until his pants were back around his waist and his cock was zipped up before speaking. I wasn't surprised. There was no clocking out in this line of work and Patrick didn't waste time when he didn't have to.

"Not exactly, but I will."

"That's funny," he said in a tone that said it was anything *but* funny, "because I sent you to get my money."

I didn't want to split hairs, but I clarified my mission. "You sent me to remind him why it was stupid *not* to pay," I said, ignoring his glare because even though he thought he was badass with the glares—which he was—he was still my father. "Five days and he'll have the money in full. Guaranteed."

"Five more days, really? And how exactly will he have the money, Eamon? Gamblers are notorious liars."

"Because I'll be checking in with him daily. He wants to pay the money back because he wants to keep working with us and I intend to make sure both of those things happen."

Patrick grinned. "That's what I love about you, son. You're always focused on the bigger picture." His grin faded back to all business. "Just make sure I have my money by the end of the week. Or else." He didn't need to emphasize the threat. I understood it loud and clear.

If the money wasn't here in five days, Peter Michaels wasn't the only one who'd be in deep shit.

Chapter Seven

Layla

The thing I loved most about my job was flex days. I had until eleven o'clock to get to work, which allowed me to do hot yoga at eight before I had to be in the office.

I *needed* hot yoga this morning, more than anyone in the history of the world has ever needed *any* kind of yoga, hot or otherwise. Eamon Connelly would expect an answer from me and I had to tell him yes. *Yeah sure, I'm gonna let you fuck me for four days straight so you'll cancel my dad's debt. What the fuck am I getting myself into?*

I'd pondered it all night long when I should have been sleeping to rest up for the full day of work I had ahead of me. What if Dad owed three or four grand? Seriously, I could pay that much to get him out of debt, but it was still a lot of money. Not that my dad's life wasn't important, but I didn't even get to have fun gambling all that money away.

I wondered, would I whore myself out for a measly two thousand bucks? What if he only owed five hundred or a thousand? Oh, God. I'd be a cheap whore without even knowing it.

Then again, what if it was more than that and it got Eamon to thinking that maybe he'd be overpaying for the fuck and he'd extend it to a week? A month? No, four days was doable. Tolerable. Anything more than that, I just couldn't stand.

I could get through four days of this. Mostly because I was a pretty tough chick, at least I liked to think I was. I'd had enough casual sex to know good sex didn't equal love. But there was something in those swirling, colorful eyes of Eamon's that told me he wouldn't fight fair. He seemed like the kind of guy who played for keeps, played dirty to make sure every woman wanted him, even though he didn't want to give them more than necessary.

He was a player in every sense of the word.

And that made me horny as fuck.

But I should know how much I was doing the deed for? Would I regret knowing my going rate?

"Ugh, stop!" I stared at myself in the mirror, smiling at the new burgundy blouse I picked out of my closet this morning. I finally ripped the price tag—there goes that word again—off and I promised myself that I'd kick my own ass if I thought about *him* one more time.

Work. I had to get to work. Today my team would start working on the official proposal for our new client and I was eager to get started. If *he* wanted to know my answer, he would find a way to get it, otherwise I was washing my hands of it.

Right now.

As of this moment.

Dammit.

Satisfied with my reflection and doubly satisfied that my attempt at cigarette pants didn't make my ass look big, I vowed that I wouldn't let anything ruin my day.

"You hear that, Universe? Nothing!"

I grabbed my bag, my purse and my phone, thinking of nothing but what my playlist would be. "Dammit, I should've kept that last part to myself." Standing on my doorstep looking as fuckable as ever in a blue three-piece suit with a light blue shirt that made him look like a model, fresh from some steamy island destination instead of the dungeon he'd probably come from.

"Good morning to you too, princess."

I wanted to smack him. "Layla. My name is Layla."

"I know your name."

Damn, this guy was what girls meant when they called someone sex on a stick. His voice pitched all low and gravelly, the tone meant to dampen panties and clench thighs. Mission accomplished, dammit.

"Then use it. Why are you here?"

"You know why I'm here."

He did it again and I nodded like some mute dummy. "You want an answer." It wasn't a question because that was the only possible reason he would show up.

"I do."

Of course he did. I stepped forward at the same time Eamon did but of course he was at least a foot taller than me, maybe more, and his steps were bigger than mine, pushing me back into the house. "You don't need to come in for the answer. I have to get to work."

"You have time." His tone was confident and that sent a shiver or maybe it was a thrill through me at the notion that he somehow knew about my flex days. "So, what'll it be, *Layla*?"

Sweet baby Jesus. The man said my name better than Eric Clapton ever could and the way his rolled his tongue around each syllable had my mind thinking about that tongue curling around *other* things. But then I remembered. This wasn't about desire, this was about possession, and it was technically commerce. I needed to remember that now more than ever. "I think you know I have to say yes."

His eyes looked like pure gold against the blue suit with tiny lightning bolts of brown to complete his *hot mob boss* look. "You don't *have* to do anything you don't want to."

"It must be nice to live such a black and white life. What I *want,* Eamon, is for my father to never have borrowed that damn money in the first place. That's what I want so don't give me that shit. You want it clear? Yes. Yes to the four days to clear the debt." I didn't miss the gleam of satisfaction in his eyes that quickly turned to desire or the twisted smirk on his *still* kissable mouth.

"Good. I'll make sure you enjoy yourself." The way he licked his lips guaranteed at least a partial good time for me. I just hoped it would be enough.

"Does it matter if I do?"

"It damn well does. When I slide my tongue deep inside that sweet wet cunt of yours and hear you scream my name, my cock will be so hard, so ready to burst." I wasn't ashamed to admit I swallowed. Hard. At the imagery. "And just to make sure you know when it happens, I'll come all over those pretty tits of yours."

Yes, please. I mean, maybe. I wasn't really a girl who went for the porn shit. I could give a good blowjob but dude juice on my tits wasn't really my thing. But to know he'd come that hard because of me? I might hate it a little less. "You have a dirty mouth." Damn, why couldn't my voice ever sound that husky when I wanted it to?

"You'll like it. Don't worry Layla, I promise to talk real dirty while I show you what I want to do to that smart mouth."

I shivered. I fucking shivered. At least I'd get some guaranteed orgasms. I liked guaranteed orgasms. A lot.

"My place, tonight at seven. I'll send a car."

And now we'd officially moved into *Pretty Woman* territory. There was no need to respond because he wasn't asking any damn questions. Only issuing orders. I was determined to be pissed about that even though it turned me on way more than it should have.

I cursed Eamon's name on my fifteen-minute-drive to work. I squeezed my knees together in the elevator just thinking about that leather and pine scent I knew was somehow all him. I cursed his name even as I made a last-minute lunchtime appointment for a full wax and buff. And a quick stop at a lingerie shop before I headed home at the end of the day.

If I was going to do this, then I'd have the armor I needed.

***

I expected that a mob boss—or whatever the other guys in the mob who *aren't* bosses—would live in some swanky condo in downtown Rocket or one of those flashy monstrosities inside the gated communities that now dotted the city. But when we drove up to the modern cement and glass structure that practically blended into the mountain behind it, I thought the driver had made a mistake. *This* was where Eamon called home? I stood inside a paved circular driveway beside the young female driver, but I couldn't see inside because of the lack of windows.

"Wait here," she instructed before turning around, getting behind the wheel and driving off.

Leaving me standing there like a creeper. More like *creepy* with the whole lack of windows thing, especially now that we were on the wrong side of the sunset thanks to his man cave of a house. Though it was modern, the house had a distinctly gothic vibe or maybe that was just the trick of the light. Or my nerves.

"Come closer, Layla. I won't bite until later."

I scanned the wall until I spotted Eamon, looking fuckable as hell in a pair of jeans and a plain white t-shirt. Fuck me, the man looked good in a suit, like extra

Good with a capital 'G' kind of good but in jeans, he was downright devastating. "I didn't want to guess where the door might be on your booby trap house."

His deep laugh sounded amused and well used, like he laughed a lot. I didn't imagine mob workers smiled all that much, but maybe Eamon really liked his job. "Come on in *princess*."

Once inside the house I was surprised by how well-lit it was. Maybe I'd been expecting a dark den of sin with gas lanterns and a creepy butler with a sloping hump in his back. But everything about the house was bright, cheerful even, which took a minute to adjust to when I was expecting red and black leather, whips, chains, sexual torture devices and guns. Couldn't forget the guns since he was a mobster, after all. "Layla." I reiterated.

"Right. Princess just seems so fitting."

"Yeah, know a lot of princesses like me, do ya?" Not that I wanted to know a damn thing about the kind of women he dated, fucked and forgot, but he was so sure of himself, so sure of who he thought I was.

"Can't say I do."

"It creeps me out. My dad calls me that."

His eyes raked over my body, slow and lazy, like a lover's caress. And we weren't lovers.

When he put his hand on his hip, the light caught on his arm and that was when I saw it. Or rather, *them*. Tattoos. Lots of them, in fact. Two partial sleeves of color and vibrant imagery. "You like the art?"

I blinked and looked at his handsome smirking face. "It's nice. Colorful and unexpected."

"Glad you approve. This way." I didn't miss his mocking tone but I chose to keep quiet. This wasn't a date. It was a debt.

I followed behind Eamon, mostly staring at his ass because it was a fine ass. Just round enough to know that he was physically fit. If I squeezed it or nibbled it, I knew both cheeks would be firm. Judging by the way the jeans hugged his thighs, he was strong enough to lift me up and fuck me against the wall. Any wall. *The wall right here. Now.*

"Cool design. Did you buy it like this?"

Eamon stopped inside a large room with two sectional sofas and plenty of art on the walls and even a few sculptures. The room was decorated in warm colors, and everything about it screamed high class. Quality. Luxury. "We don't have to do this, Layla. The small talk."

"Right." I straightened my spine and removed the black jacket I grabbed on my way out the door. Since we were doing that whole *Pretty Woman* thing, it revealed the short red strapless dress I wore underneath. It was short and tight and my boobs were barely stuffed into it, but the look in his eyes right now was totally worth the discomfort and acrobatics I'd needed to get into it.

"Nice dress." His voice was dark and thick with desire and when I looked down, his cock was straining to get out of his jeans. I may have clenched a little.

"No small talk," I reminded him as I slid one hand down the side of my dress in search of the zipper. I found the tiny gold tab and tugged it down, slowly until it stopped at my hip, leaving me to find a graceful way out of it. Luckily this wasn't my first time performing a striptease for a guy. I let the fabric fall into a pool around my feet, stepped out of it and kicked it away. "Will here do?" There was a plush carpet in front of a freestanding fireplace and a sectional just close enough that the fire would keep two naked bodies perfectly warm, maybe even sweaty once things got going.

"What do you think you're doing?"

Okay, now I was the one who was confused. "If you don't want small talk then clearly you want to get right to the fucking, right?" There were no other options and now that I'd finally gotten my courage up to accept this, he wanted to play games. Because, men.

"There will be fucking, don't you worry about that. My cock is so hard right now just thinking about pounding into your tight little cunt, but don't think you can manipulate your way out of this." In an instant his gaze went from dark and playful to dark, dangerous and sobering. I could see the gangster within him and it thrilled me as much as it terrified me.

"Eamon, I'm confused. You don't want to talk and you don't want to fuck, so what am I doing here? And in brand new lingerie, I might add."

"Eager?"

Resigned was more accurate, but I didn't think saying so would get the evening off to the right start. So I searched for a more appropriate word and came up with one. "Prepared."

"Likes and dislikes?"

"Chocolate and assholes."

He glared.

I smiled and raised my eyebrows. "I'll let you know either way."

"Do that. If you can talk." His words shouldn't have made my knees go wobbly, but they did. I'd never met a man who could say so much without hardly saying a thing and have it all sound so fucking dirty.

I'd make sure I could talk because if he could make me forget myself, lose myself to him, there would be trouble. I'd engage but Eamon would be like any other one—uh, *four*—night stand. Memorable for the pleasure and the weird sexy things that happened between naked bodies and nothing more.

Without another word, I sucked in a deep breath and slid my hands over my hips and up the curve of my waist, cupping my boobs until my fingers wrapped around the front clasp. One flick of the wrist and the intricate black lace opened, baring my boobs for his view. His judgment. I had nice tits, a solid D cup that was a bit too big for my frame but I'd never had any complaints. Still, every quirk of his lips looked like he had assessed me and found me lacking in some way, so I stood and stared at him for a long moment.

His gaze lingered on my chest until first my left nipple hardened and then tightened into a stiff bead that was almost painful. Then he worked the same eye magic on the right one, smiling when two rosy nipples were hard enough to cut glass.

"Leave them on," he barked out when my fingers dipped inside the waistband of the lacy black thong.

"Lie down." He moved aside to the end of the sectional sofa and motioned right where he wanted me.

I wanted to tell him to go fuck himself. To tell him to say please or something else sarcastic and inane but I couldn't because my legs, the little sluts, were carrying me right where Eamon wanted me. I sat and leaned back, feeling clinical like I was lying on a paper covered slab in the gyno's office and I kept my gaze on the ceiling just like I did while my doctor tried to make small talk, like I wanted to talk about the weather when he was elbow deep into my lady parts.

"Spread your legs."

I did and immediately sucked in a breath as the cool air hit the warm, wet area between my thighs. If someone would've asked me an hour ago how I felt about being ordered around in the bedroom, I would have got up in their face and told them that no guy was the boss of me. But that deep baritone that brooked no argument didn't just do it for me, it made me *want* to obey. How fucked up was that?

Eamon smiled. "Already wet and I haven't even touched you."

"I was thinking about Chris Hemsworth on the way over to make sure we had all systems go."

His laugh sounded deeper and closer and then I felt the heat of his body against my leg. "Whatever you need to tell yourself, Layla. But you and I know the truth, don't we?" He didn't wait for an answer, just dragged two knuckles right against my wet panties until I gasped. "Wider."

I opened my legs until I was indecent, feeling even more arousal seep out of me at his intense, wanton gaze. His eyes looked black from here, his breathing shallow and his fist clenched as his gaze washed over me. I realized that my body had a mind of its own where Eamon was concerned. His gaze had me so close to orgasm, I tried to remember why this was a bad idea, why I was mad about being here. Only I couldn't.

"Better." Then he sat one knee between my legs and leaned over until our bodies were aligned from lips to hips. Too bad he was fully dressed because my pussy throbbed for more than a simple look. But the way Eamon kissed was damn near better than sex.

He held my face like guys do to women who were precious to them, tight and possessive, while his mouth plundered my own. His tongue swiped across my lips, darting inside at my first intake of breath and then he set my whole body on fire with just his mouth. Even his hands, strong capable hands, did little more than hold me in place for his mouth to fuck mine, because that's what it turned into. Fucking. His tongue slicked and flicked, tasted and taunted my mouth, playful and intense. Then he pulled back. "These tits. Perfect."

I was raised with manners and wanted to thank him for the compliment but when that mouth, with the thicker bottom lip, wrapped around my still hard nipple, my brain functioning ceased.

Totally fucking stopped.

All I could do was feel the glide of his tongue over the hard bead, the press of his teeth into the soft flesh of my breast, the combination when he sucked, hard until I arched into him. "Fuck," I moaned when he blew on my nipple before giving the other breast the same exact treatment. While he teased me, his fingers found my other sensitive, slick nipple and pinched until it hurt.

I wanted to tell him to stop, that it was too much, but then I felt it, the stream of moisture gathering between my thighs. It was more than too much but in the best possible way.

"Fucking perfect."

I didn't know why he'd left my breasts but they felt cold without him and my own hands replaced his while Eamon kissed his way down my torso, licking the warm strip of flesh under my breast and down my ribcage, dipping his tongue inside my belly button before he plucked the waistband of my panties with his teeth.

Then he buried his face between my legs. And inhaled. I wanted to be grossed out, but the vibrations shook my entire body, making my clit stand up and take notice. "Oh, shit."

He looked up at me, a totally sensual but smug look in his face as his tongue snaked out, the tip teasing me mercilessly in quick, barely there figure eights.

"Oh shit is close, but not quite what I was going for," he said.

Then he opened his mouth and began to French kiss my pussy through my panties. It was dirty and it was erotic and I fucking loved it.

His tongue, hell his whole mouth was a thing of beauty. A wizard who could, with a flick of his tongue, render intelligent women stupid. Who could perform exorcisms with nothing more than simple suck? Who could make me wetter than I'd ever been in my entire life, even during my weekend long spank sessions?

"Oh fuck, yeah! Yes, Eamon!"

Those words snapped something inside him because he grabbed the side of my panties and pulled them from my body, and then he was pleasing me again, only this time it was the soft feel of his lips on me, the slight scratch from his stubble on my thighs, my pussy. He pushed my legs so far apart it was uncomfortable but what he was doing to me, the sounds he pulled from me were the result of so much fucking pleasure that he could have dislocated my hips for all it mattered.

"God, yes!" My hips began to move as he slid is tongue inside of me, fucking me hard with his tongue while his nose bumped against my clit over and over and over again.

"Eamon, oh Eamon, yes!" My whole body drew up tight for several long seconds before a powerful and intense orgasm worked its way up my limbs and out of every pore of my body. I shook. My body trembled. My mouth let out an embarrassing wailing keen that I couldn't stop.

"Fuck, I knew you'd be a screamer," he growled and got up beside me, whipping out his cock, his long thick cock, pumped it a few times and then came all over my tits and stomach. "And a squirter," he said darkly and licked his lips.

Yeah, I shivered at that because apparently, I was a dirty slut. "Wow. That's never happened to me before." Because if it had, my brain would have been working properly and I wouldn't have shared that bit of intel that would only pump up his ego even more.

Eamon stood at the side of the sofa and slowly removed his t-shirt to reveal a chest covered with lickable, indescribable muscles.

With his cock back in his hand making my mouth water, Eamon stroked himself and smiled. "Then let's see if we can make you do it again."

I had a feeling that all the thoughts I had about Eamon were true. Fucking was sport for him and I needed to remember that when his fucking felt a lot like something else.

Something deeper.

Something real.

It probably should have scared the shit out of me. None of this was real. My flesh, my body was nothing more than a means of debt collection. He wanted to fuck me, to debase me and he had no problem using whatever means he could to make it happen.

And my dad, the man who was supposed to protect me, had given him just that.

KB Winters

Chapter Eight

Eamon

"Tell me Layla, are you cock hungry?" I knelt beside her on the sofa, watching her body respond to my every word. Every reaction. At the question her breath hitched, her blue eyes darkened until they were nearly black but not quite. Glazed with desire. Then her tongue slicked across her lips and I knew I was right. "You *are* cock hungry." But it was more than that, between the licking and sucking, she was turned up and all it would take was a flick of my tongue, a glide of my finger over her pussy and she'd explode.

Her plump lips spread into a dirty grin as her hand reached out to me and wrapped around my recently spent cock.

"I might be, but if not, let's just say I'm motivated to get this big boy ready to go again."

The way she said it, with awe and reverence in her voice, helped things along. My cock grew longer and harder as she stroked, looking at my cock like it was her favorite ice cream and today was her cheat day.

I smiled. "Big boy?"

One blonde brow arched up at me.

"Fishing for compliments? I would've thought a man like you knew exactly the gift he had."

I couldn't get any fucking words out when she squeezed and stroked my cock while the other cupped my balls in her warm hand.

"Fine. You have a nice big cock, Eamon. But my favorite part is how thick it is, how when I squeeze just enough," her hands did what her mouth said, "he gets just a little thicker."

Then to drive her point home, she held me and licked me from the bottom of my sac to the tip of my cock, pulling a shiver from me.

When Layla licked her lips for a third time, a low moan escaped from somewhere deep inside of me. There was no fucking way in hell I was gonna blow my load on a hand job, something I hadn't done since Mary

Rose in the eighth grade, no matter how good it felt in her soft capable hands.

"Layla." There it went again, the hitched breath when I said her name, turning my cock to hardened steel.

She rolled on to her stomach so that her face was eye level with my dick.

"Yes?" The little tease smiled up at me. "Is this what you want?"

She gave my cock two rough tugs and then took me in her mouth, gripping my thighs hard.

"Oh fuck!" Her mouth was warm, no it was hot as fuck and wet, and so goddamn deep I wondered when I would find the back of her throat.

"Shit, princess."

I smirked at her response, taking me deeper until my legs trembled and a sheen of sweat broke out all over my body. She started slow, basically kissing my cock and using plenty of tongue, which I appreciated. But soon she went all in, gripping me tight in her hand

and hollowing her cheeks as she took me deep. So fucking deep I could feel the muscles in my legs tense.

Layla handled my cock like a pro. Her hands were never idle as she licked and sucked like it was an ice pop on a hot Nevada day. One hand stayed on my balls, cupping and squeezing just enough to send ripples of awareness sling-shotting through me while the other gripped my ass, urging me deeper.

And deeper.

She moaned around my cock as if she was getting as much pleasure from eating my dick as I was, and my control snapped. Grabbing Layla by a fistful of hair, I yanked her back, away from my cock.

"Let's pick that up later," I told her roughly and she looked up at me with wide, wild eyes, letting me move her around the sofa by her hair until she was flat on her back with her legs wide open, giving me the perfect view of her slick cunt.

"Oh-oh-okay," she stammered and for some reason that had me growing ever harder. Thicker.

Several beads of pre-come made my dickhead slick and shiny and I could tell how bad she wanted it. I loved a cock hungry bitch. "Take it."

She looked up at me, confused and all kinds of turned on. Then she smiled, turned her head and opened her mouth for me.

"Yeah, cock hungry." I shoved my cock in her mouth roughly because I wanted to see how she would handle it. Disappointment flashed for a brief moment when her hand went to my thigh but then the dirty girl pulled me closer, urged me deeper into her mouth. Down her throat.

I didn't know how long I fucked that gorgeous little mouth, but I fucked it the same way I planned to fuck her pussy, hard and fast. My hips pumped faster with every swipe of her tongue and she took it, flattening her tongue in an effort to make me lose my fucking mind. Even the wet, gagging noises didn't stop me. Or her.

Nothing could stop me, not when she took it all and silently begged for more. But when that little pink tongue snuck out and swiped the underside of my sac, all was lost. "What the ... oh, fuck!"

Quick as lightning, I pulled my cock from her mouth and flipped her over so her chest was flat against the sofa, heart shaped ass in the air aimed my way, tempting me. Teasing me. Fucking taunting me. I would have her ass, but not tonight. In one hard thrust I was deep inside the fiery lava of her wet pussy, giving her a moment to adjust to my size. "Goddamn, you have a tight little pussy, Layla."

"Fuck!" She panted the word, her walls squeezing me, enticing me to move before she was ready.

I didn't want to take my time, I wanted to pound into her hard and fast, but we had three more days and I wanted her to be ready for me. Every. Fucking. Day.

"So fucking tight," I told her as I pulled nearly all the way out and pushed back in. Again and again until the only sounds she made were loud, shrill and incoherent.

"Such a wet fuckin' cunt. Soaked just for me."

Every dirty word from my mouth made her pussy clench and squeeze so hard I thought she might push me out completely.

"Oh fuck yeah! Eamon." She moaned my name like it was the only goddamn word in her vocabulary, pussy pulsing because she was close. "Yeah? You like it when I fuck you hard and deep like this?"

The pace wasn't fast but I fucked her deep. Every thrust pushing her and the sofa away from me, and when she reached for me, I grabbed her wrists and pinned them behind her back.

"Eamon?" The question was equal parts desire, fear and wariness. Good, she should be wary.

"Don't worry princess, you'll like it when I hold you down and fuck you. If you don't, let me know."

But I knew she wouldn't. Gripping her forearms with a forceful tug, I slid my dick in and out of her, hard and fast and deep while she squirmed and moaned and screamed her fucking pleasure.

Then she was coming. Hard. Strangling my dick to the point of pain but I didn't give a shit, not when her body convulsed so hard it milked me dry in one long pulse.

"Oh, oh, oh yesssss!" she screamed.

Another tidal wave slammed against her, pulling her under while I continued fucking her until my cock was too soft to stay inside her, until my nuts were completely spent.

I smacked her ass and collapsed on top of her. "Fuck me, I can fuck that pussy all night long."

Layla laughed, a husky amused sound as she looked at me over her shoulder. "Never received a compliment like that before, but thanks."

I smacked her ass and pulled back, separating our sticky bodies as the cool air hit us. "Take a shower if you want but don't think about leaving or putting on clothes."

It took her a minute but Layla finally turned over and stood, shaking out her limbs with a satisfied smile.

"A shower sounds nice," she said and turned to me with a question in her beautiful blue eyes. "Where would the bathroom be?"

"Right. Through the master bedroom at the end of the hall." I didn't feel the need to follow her or show her where anything was because I knew women. She'd snoop, it was inevitable and just like the others, she would walk away disappointed. This was my home but mostly it was just where I laid my head at night, had a meal once in a while. It wasn't where I kept anything important, not to a woman anyway.

I just hoped she didn't piss me off before I had my fill of her, not if I would be on the hook for her father's debt. Layla was a freak and she was the best fucking kind, an undiscovered freak and I needed to fuck her until she couldn't walk. I had to. She was more than a tight cunt with a tighter body, she was that rare woman who actually loved to fuck. She didn't just tolerate it because she got all that came along with it, no Layla loved a good fuck. Threw herself into it and best of all, the kinkier and dirtier it was, the more turned on and wet she became.

The sound of the shower turned on quickly, surprising me since I'd expected her to spend a few minutes snooping while the water warmed up. The thought of the water slicking over those curves and thinking that maybe she was thinking of me and touching herself, had my feet on the move and heading toward the master bathroom. "Need some help?"

She sucked in a breath at the intrusion and turned to me with a smile. "There are a few hard to reach spots you could help me with."

And just like that, I was ready to go again with Layla's legs wrapped around my waist as I fucked her hard under the waterfall shower spray. There was no foreplay and no preamble, just a good hard fuck that had us both coming in under a minute. "Fuck!" The word came out as a loud roar as I shot my load into her screaming, quivering body.

"Not sure I can walk after that," she said with a low, throaty tone.

"Don't worry, the bed is just a few feet away and I'm happy to carry you there and keep you there." For the night.

And the next four fucking days.

***

"Not that I'm complaining, but if we keep this up I'm going to need a saline drip to hydrate my body." Layla smiled the smile of a woman who'd been well fucked. Her blonde hair was mussed from my hands, gripping it while I fucked her mouth, her pussy and even while I kissed her until she clenched around my fingers.

I went to the kitchen and came back with two bottles of water, handing one to her. "Can't have you dehydrated when I need you dripping wet, can I?"

Her little pink tongue snaked out and licked her lips, telling me she liked what she was hearing. "That would be tragic," she said, her tone joking.

"You're different than I thought you'd be." Where the fuck did those words come from?

"Yeah, tell me."

I shrugged because the cat was already out of the fucking bag, so why not? "I thought you were some spoiled college girl who'd make this arrangement miserable because of the circumstances."

Her smile dimmed and I wondered if I'd said too much. "First of all I wish I was spoiled. If not for a full academic scholarship I'd probably be waiting tables at one of the casinos in Rocket."

"And second?"

"Would it do me any good to make this situation worse by complaining? You're a good fuck which helps me forget, well at least until you brought it up."

Right. "Well we can talk about something else."

"As long as it's not small talk?" She laughed before I could reply, waving away the reply on my lips good-naturedly. "I do have a question."

"Yes, I'll be ready to go again in a few minutes," I told her and thrust my hips against the side of her leg, appreciating that she didn't misinterpret what tonight was. There was a respectable distance between us on the bed, naked.

"How much money does my dad owe you?" At my silence she pressed on. "I've already agreed to this so whether it's a few hundred or a few grand, it doesn't matter anymore, right?"

I could tell she wanted to know, hell she probably needed to know considering what she was giving up to get the damn debt paid. "Knowing won't make it any easier."

"Maybe, but it can't make it any harder, can it?" The way she said it gave me pause. I knew she was enjoying herself, her screams and her body didn't lie, but was that just based on circumstance?

"Is this hard?"

"It's not easy, but at least the dick is damn good." She made an effort at a genuine smile but it wasn't, dammit. "Is this your way of changing the subject?"

"Your father has a serious gambling problem, Layla."

She sighed and blew out a deep breath before turning those large emerald eyes onto me. "So I've gathered. How long have you known him?"

"Years. He's been doing business with us for years." At first he never borrowed more than a few grand at a time but over the past few years it had only gotten worse, a fact I didn't want to burden her with. Not right now when I wanted to fuck her.

"Years? And stupid me thinking he was depressed and drowning his sorrows in booze when it was worse. So much worse."

She covered her face with her hands and I wondered if I was going to have to console a crying woman instead of fucking her.

"I'm such an idiot. No wonder you don't think much of me."

"Lay—,"

"No, I didn't say that for a compliment. It doesn't matter but what does matter to me is his debt. How much is it?"

"Why do you want to know?"

"Because I'm paying this stupid debt with my body and I deserve to know how much it is."

And that was the one point I couldn't argue. "Forty grand. Forty-three and a half to be precise."

She sucked in a breath as my words sank in, her eyes so wide I thought they might pop right out of her head. "Holy fuck. Why would you even loan him that amount of money?"

Here it came, the berating, like it was the fault of the Connelly family that her dad couldn't handle his shit. "Because everyone always pays."

Her head nodded absently as she processed my words. "Yeah, I get that. But what about my broke-ass dad made you think he could ever pay back so much money?"

"Like I said, everyone always pays. One way or another. If they can't come up with the cash then they run errands, make deliveries or do whatever we need done until my father says the debt is clear. Sometimes we put them to work on the streets selling ass, making risky deliveries or gathering intel. There are plenty of ways to repay a debt, Layla."

"No kidding." The words were weighted with a heaviness I didn't like.

"Don't ever follow your old man's footsteps honey, you have a shitty poker face."

Layla shrugged, drawing my attention to the delicate curve of her neck. "I wasn't trying to mask anything," she said honestly.

I knew exactly what she was thinking. Wondering how many other times I'd cashed in a debt with pussy.

I never did it because I didn't have to; women were basic creatures. They either wanted to fuck a rich guy in hopes of it leading to a long-term relationship, or they wanted to fuck a hot guy because they were in search of a night or two of pleasure. And I was both.

"Those thoughts aren't helpful, princess."

She stiffened beside me and turned her gaze to mine. "You can't possibly know what I'm thinking or if it'll help."

"You're wondering how many times I've done this."

Layla looked at me and burst out laughing. "God, you are even more arrogant than you seem. I was thinking that if I made forty grand for four days of work, I'd be a rich woman right now."

Okay, I hadn't expected that. "So you're saying I should add a few more days?"

"No," she grinned. "I'm just wondering if I would've been a successful hooker."

For some reason I didn't want to examine too closely, I didn't like Layla thinking of herself like that. She wasn't a hooker, she was a woman doing what needed to be done to save someone she cared about. That was the Connelly way and I respected the hell out of her for it. But clearly, the night was over. "I have an early morning tomorrow so you should probably head home. My driver is waiting downstairs for you and she'll pick you up tomorrow at the same time."

Layla froze for a brief second and then, instead of reacting or responding, she left the bed and then the bedroom. I paused, waiting to hear grumbling or maybe even the sound of something breaking but there was nothing but silence. Not even the hint of a rustle of clothing as she got dressed.

Strange. I got off the bed and strode butt naked into the living room to catch her snooping, but she wasn't snooping, damn her. Nope, Layla had gathered her clothes into a pile, picking up each article and sliding it on in total silence. "You okay?"

"Yep. Fine." Fine, the universal female word for *not fucking fine at all* but since she wasn't my problem, I didn't ask again. But I watched her step into her panties and pull them up her fine legs until they were settled on her hips. Next was the bra and finally the dress. She didn't dress with as much care as I was sure she had at the start of the evening but it went quickly. She slipped on her coat, picked up her shoes and purse before turning to me. "Goodnight."

That was it. No kiss to keep me interested, no longing looks that said she might be getting the wrong idea. Just a bland farewell that I wanted, hell expected.

But somehow it left me feeling unsatisfied.

Layla Michaels wasn't at all what I expected in the best possible way and I couldn't wait until tomorrow.

Because tomorrow, she'd be mine again, all night long.

KB Winters

Chapter Nine

Layla

Stupid. So fucking stupid. That was how I felt as I climbed into the back of the limo, which now held a distinctively cool air. Stupid. Like a stupid, fucking whore. And Eamon Connelly had made me feel that way.

That asshole.

But was he the real asshole or was I the asshole who allowed him to make me feel this way? I knew what this was, a quick hard fuck to pay back a debt. No more and no fucking less. But here I was feeling like I'd been used. Well used and in the best possible way but still, his mood changes made my head spin.

That was the thing no one ever said about good— no great—sex. That the intensity and the hormones can confuse even the smartest of women into thinking— mistakenly—that some kind of connection was taking place when it wasn't. The only things connecting were our bodies, wet and panting, until the pleasure became too much to bear and had to escape our bodies in what can only be described as the perfect orgasm. And if I was smart, I'd have gotten up as soon as the last shiver left my body and got the hell out of dodge.

But the shower sex had been memorable. Not just memorable but unforgettable. It was so hot and hard with the addition of the steam and water, the rawness of it had been hot as fuck. A shiver shot through me in the back of the limo at the thought of that encounter. But like men do, Eamon had to go and ruin it by reminding me he was a world-class asshole.

It was a good reminder for me though, because there were times back there that I really *felt* a connection and I tried not to make too many connections. Some shrink would probably say it had to do with losing my mom at such a pivotal age and they might've been right, but that only made the connection I felt more disconcerting.

I'd just keep reminding myself that the guy he was *after* he'd fucked me, was who Eamon Connelly really was. He wasn't some good guy, he was just a good lay. This wasn't some love affair and it wasn't even a proper booty call. I was in his bed, on his sofa and in his shower because I had to be. To clear Dad's debt.

This was a paid fuck, plain and simple. No matter how nice he may have seemed or how much he charmed me, I needed to remember what this arrangement really was. A business transaction.

Nothing more.

Which is why I spent the rest of the limo ride back to my place, catching up on the day's news on my phone. Okay, the week's news because work kept me busy and when it didn't, making sure Dad was taken care of did and I didn't get a lot of time to myself. The time I did get was usually spent watching reality TV and crime documentaries.

But there was a lot going on in the world, some of it was a hell of a lot more interesting than what was going on in my life. No matter how dark and twisted it was. I got absorbed in world events until the limo came to a halt outside my apartment building. I hopped out before the pixie driver had a chance to remove her seatbelt, hurrying up the stairs and inside my building just in case the little fairy thought of doing something crazy like walking me to my door.

Thankfully, the halls and the elevator were empty so I could do my walk of shame without an audience. Not that I felt much shame.

Anger? Yeah.

Humiliation? Double yeah.

Homicidal? Fuck yeah.

But I was home now and day one was over with, which meant I was that much closer to the end of my ... sentence? Billing cycle?

Whatever it was, we were one day closer to the end of this little game. When I was less frustrated, I might examine why that didn't make me as happy as it should, but I was exhausted and nothing but a hot bath and a glass of something strong and dark would cure it.

Chapter Ten

Eamon

Another reason I didn't mess around with good girls? They made a guy feel bad when he had no damn reason to feel anything of the sort. I hadn't done anything wrong to Layla. I didn't break any promises and I didn't mistreat her, yet here I was feeling like an asshole watching the limo carry her away.

Until tomorrow.

Tonight though, tonight I had other business and as soon as she was out of my eyesight I went back to my room and got dressed in jeans and a sweater because nighttime in Rocket could be cold as shit. Even though I enjoyed receiving payment tonight from Layla, I couldn't be sure her old man had gotten the message. It wouldn't be the first time Peter Michaels had said one thing and done another, which meant I had to put on my game face and show him that I meant business.

That my family meant fucking business.

I hopped on my bike and made my way back to the shitty little apartment he now called home after selling the house Layla had grown up in to feed his gambling habit. Retracing my steps from earlier, I stopped at the top landing, pulled out my phone and called my driver. "Did Ms. Michaels make it home safely?"

"She did, about twenty minutes ago. I stayed like you asked and she hasn't left again."

"Thanks, Gigi. Watch another ten minutes and tell me if anything changes. If it doesn't, you can head home for the night."

"Got it, Boss. Later."

I rolled my eyes because I hated that she always called me boss like we were factory workers in the 1940's. Without another word, I ended the call and stopped on the faded black mat in front of Peter Michaels' apartment. I raised my fist and knocked hard, feeling wound up and angry that I was back here again because it made me think of the last visit.

Me pounding the fuck out of him.

Layla strolling inside and trying to protect her father.

A hot fucking mess.

"Yeah, whaddya want ... oh, Mr. Connelly?" The son of a bitch had the audacity to roll his eyes as if I was the one inconveniencing him.

"What do I want? What I want is for you to pay what we were so gracious to loan you in the first place, but since you haven't, I thought we needed to have a little talk."

He stumbled back with a grunt, stinking of booze and sweat, red glassy eyes not leaving me for even a second. Smart even if he couldn't do jack shit about it.

"Didn't we have a talk already, the one where your fists talked to my face until I understood you were pissed about the money? Not that your family even needs the money. It's probably a drop in the bucket compared to your wealth."

He snorted, shaking his head like we were the bad guys.

The Connelly family was no group of innocents, but we had honor. Without fucking honor, a man, a family didn't have shit.

"It's not about how much we have, Michaels, it's about how much we loaned to you. When you needed it. Now we want it back."

My gaze swept over the sparsely furnished living room, and I took a seat on the dingy sofa that I somehow knew Layla made sure was clean.

"In fact, I seem to remember giving you every opportunity to go home and sleep it off, but you refused, so sure your cold streak was about to end."

It was the story of every gambler's life, fucking hot and cold streaks, like there was some way to predict luck. When it came and when it dried up was as random as anything else but the pull, the thrill of the win was too fucking powerful for some.

His shoulders fell and he hung his head low. "I do and I appreciate you for it, but if I could have gone home then I would have."

"And what about now? Am I going to find you back at one of my offices begging for money again?"

Peter's eyes darted all around the room. Everywhere but at me. I knew the answer by the way his fingers twitched like there were cards or chips in front of him. "Layla would kill me."

"And you're already trying to think of what gaming rooms might loan you money, only hours after your daughter finished paying down a part of your debt?"

His eyes went wide with shock, surprise and maybe even a little disgust, which only confirmed my suspicions that Layla hadn't told him about our deal. She could have. Hell, she should have, used it as leverage to get him into a treatment program or to guilt him into quitting altogether. But she hadn't. Another interesting fact to store away for later.

"Leave Layla out of this," he said. "She has nothing to do with our deal."

"But she does now," I told him.

A look of absolute horror crossed his face and I smiled, because it seemed like the fucker was finally getting it through his thick skull.

"To save you from ... me, I guess. Layla has given herself to me for four sensual days. Or nights I guess is more appropriate, if you know what I'm saying."

In a rare show of masculinity, Michaels' eyes flared with anger and he lunged at me but stumbled before he reached me. Stupid fuck.

"You rotten bastard, keep your hands off my daughter! She has nothing to do with this, damn you!"

"Thanks to you, I've had my first taste of sweet little Layla, so sweet and so ripe."

I licked my lips for good measure but the minute I closed my eyes her image was there, dressed hiked up around her waist, legs spread wide to take me. She was hot as shit with her head thrown back in lust, giving her whole self over to pure sexual pleasure. It was hot as fuck and I wanted more.

"I can't imagine giving that up."

"What about if I find a way to get you the money? If I do that, will you stop this thing with Layla?"

His green eyes pleaded with me and for the first time he actually seemed to regret his actions.

"Connelly, come on, be reasonable."

There was no way in hell I was giving up the rest of my nights with Layla. No. Fucking. Way. But I'd been known to be reasonable on occasion which is why I did something I rarely did. Show compassion.

"Can you come up with the money before the week is up?"

His shoulders slumped pitifully. "I can damn well try."

He stumbled again, eyes glassy but as sharp as he was capable of. "I'll do anything to keep Layla out of your greedy clutches."

"Anything except pay the debt owed to my family?"

Because the truth of the matter was, despite the deal I'd made with her, despite everything I'd done to her sexy body just minutes ago, none of this would have happened if he'd done what the fuck he was supposed to in the first place.

Peter scrubbed a hand over his face, looking more exhausted than I'd ever seen the man.

"Yeah, well life kind of happens, doesn't it? But you could have taken any form of payment."

"I could have," I reminded him. "And I did."

It wasn't like there weren't at least a thousand other ways I could have gotten the money back, but that wasn't the point.

"But that was on you. Had you paid your debt or at least continued to make payments on it, the need to have your sweet little girl in my bed would have been moot."

"So if I give you what's in my pockets now?"

I laughed. "It's too late for that, old man. Give me something significant, a show of good faith and maybe

I'll decide that one night with your beautiful daughter was enough."

"You're a real bastard, you know that, Connelly?"

"Thanks. Be sure to tell my old man that when you see him. But you should hope you don't because that would spell trouble for you. The kind not even Layla could save you from."

It wasn't a threat, just a fact that we both knew too well.

Patrick was still a tough son of a bitch with an iron grip on the Connelly Family. He didn't suffer fools of any kind and when he felt he'd been wronged or his family name tarnished, he handled the threat swiftly and ruthlessly.

Michaels turned to begging. "I'll do what I can, Connelly. Just please, please don't hurt my little girl."

"I don't want to hurt her. Worry about getting your hands on some cash without borrowing money from anyone else."

"I'll do my best."

That pulled a laugh from me. "Your best? Isn't that how we all ended up in this situation to start with?"

There was no need to be an asshole, to pour salt into the wound but it was too easy with guys like Michaels. Even knowing what his precious daughter was doing for him, wasn't enough to get rid of that itch to go gamble. I'd bet my new Ferrari sitting back in my garage that he was already thinking of late night games where he could find some action to put a dent in his debt.

"You don't give a shit how I pay you, Connelly, as long as you get your money."

"You're right about that Petey, but just remember that the next person you gamble with might not be as willing to negotiate as the Connelly family is. You might find yourself and your daughter doing things far, far worse."

I let those words be the last he heard from me, because he needed to remove his head from his ass before he got himself and Layla hurt.

Make no mistake, the Connelly family wasn't warm and fuzzy. We'd never been nice and sweet. Sure, we had family dinners on Sunday with lots of food and plenty of talking over one another. We loved each other with everything inside of us. But we were all ruthless and completely loyal to the family, which meant we'd do anything to protect it.

That didn't mean I wasn't sympathetic to Layla's position with a deadbeat father who would never bring her anything but pain.

I would happily use her body because that was what I did, but I hoped it was a price she'd never have to pay again.

Chapter Eleven

Layla

After tossing and turning all night, thanks in part to Eamon's Jekyll and Hyde routine, I woke up the next morning feeling different somehow. Not the kind of different where I'd wake up and the sky was bluer and the air crisper. No, this was the kind of different where I knew I needed to take the reins of my life once and for all.

That meant trying to find some semblance of control in a situation where I had none. I was stuck with Eamon for three more days and I'd deal with it, but that didn't mean I couldn't find out exactly what the hell Dad had been up to all these years. He may have thought he could hide from me like he'd done my whole life. But I was tenacious and determined to get answers.

After a quick shower, I took a minute to stretch out my poor, aching muscles before I got dressed and called Ross to let him know I wouldn't be in the office until a little later in the day. Thankfully, I had the world's coolest boss. He knew I was a hard worker who'd more than make up any time I missed. I wasn't a damn slacker and I made sure my boss, my clients, and my team knew I didn't tolerate slackers, either.

I needed answers. I realized those answers might not make me feel any better, and I knew they damn well wouldn't change anything. But still, I had to know. How deep was Dad into debt and was it just to Eamon's family? Or would I find another thug smacking the hell out of him next week?

My first stop was a visit to one of Dad's old drinking buddies. I'd known Larry since I was about twelve years old. He and his wife had been staples at family barbecues and potluck dinners, and after Mom died, they'd always invited us for Thanksgiving and Christmas. Once I hit high school, though, everything had changed. But I'd been too self-centered, too focused on how I would get out of Rocket and make a name for myself that I never really noticed how significant that change was.

Or to question why it had even happened.

Today I needed to know, so I stopped to fill up my tank and grab some coffee and a big blueberry muffin from the gas station before taking the forty-five-minute drive to Larry's house. Though calling it a house was a bit of an understatement, I realized as I made my way down the long winding path off the main road. It looked like a massive ski lodge rather than a private residence.

"We're not buyin'."

I'd barely set one foot out of the car when I heard the familiar, gruff voice I'd known for years. I turned to the man I'd affectionately called Uncle Larry with a smile on my face.

"It's a good thing I'm not selling Girl Scout Cookies or I could prove to you just how wrong you are, Uncle Larry."

He squinted and then blinked, bending low and shielding his gaze from the sun. "Layla? Is that you?"

"Sure is. Do you have a minute?" I held my breath and waited for him to scowl and tell me to get the hell off his stoop. Why I thought I might get that kind of greeting I couldn't say, only that in the past forty-eight hours I'd come to realize just how much was going on around me that I hadn't been aware of. That kind of thing had a way of shaking a girl to her core.

"Well, I'll be damned. Layla Michaels. How the hell are you, girl? Come on in." He flashed a wide, mischievous grin. "Unfortunately, Alicia isn't home right now, but come on in. You're welcome any time."

Larry stepped aside so I could enter the huge foyer.

"This place is gorgeous, Uncle Larry. Did you carve these details into the wood?"

My very first memory of Larry was watching him whittle a ballerina for me out of piece of wood. He'd been working with wood for as long as I'd known him and it looked like he'd had a big hand in making his retirement dream into a reality. I followed him into the kitchen as he filled me in on the years since I'd seen him.

"You know I did. Took damn near forever, but every day I look at it, I think, this is all mine. I worked hard for it and nobody can take it away."

His face was pink and healthy for his age and shone with pride, and his eyes glittered with excitement. "So what brings you by? Haven't seen you in a while."

I nodded at the truth of his words, jogging my memory for the last time I'd seen Uncle Larry and Aunt Alicia. "You guys showed up to my graduation. I saw you in the back but after I got my diploma you were gone."

"Things were strained back then between me and your father, but we couldn't let your big day pass without showing up. You looked so beautiful and smart up there, kid. We were as proud of you as if you were our very own."

I remember seeing them in the back row, clapping and whistling and smiling. It was like having three parents instead of one. "It meant a lot to me that you were there."

"Us too. But that's not why you're here. What's going on kiddo?"

"Well," I sighed. "Dad is in some real trouble and I recently learned that I don't know a damn thing about his life or what's been going on for most of mine."

Larry smiled and stood, grabbed two longnecks from the fridge and twisted the cap off one before handing it to me. "You were just a kid. The fact that you were oblivious was a blessing to you and your parents."

Yeah, maybe, but right now it was helping no one. "It was but now I can't help but feel like a failure because Dad owes a lot of money. I mean a lot of it, Uncle Larry, and to the wrong kind of people."

Larry whistled. "I was always worried about that. In fact, that's what tore your dad and me apart. We used to go out, gamble a little, you know, a little fun here and there. But Pete got so bad looking for the big win, he didn't ever want to stop and eventually, he just didn't stop. Ever. Before your mom passed, he was a great guy. But losing her was hard on him. He tried to hold it together, for you. Then came more gambling, more drinking. I couldn't do it." He paused and pain flashed in his eyes. "I shouldn't be telling you this. I'm sure you have enough on your plate."

He sounded so sad and torn up about it that I found myself putting my arm around him to comfort him.

"I should've tried harder dammit."

"No," I insisted. "There was nothing you could have done. According to a reliable source, he's been going on like this since I started high school and it only got worse when I left for college."

Shit, it burned my tongue to even say that out loud. "I didn't know. How could I not know?"

Uncle Larry took a swig of his beer. "It wasn't your job to know, Layla. You were just a kid. You were supposed to be doing kid things. Studying, going to the mall with your friends. You know, kid things." He took another pull of his beer and let out a long, hard breath. "What can I do to help?"

I wanted to ask him for the money. Badly. It was clear he could afford it, and given the guilt written all over his face, he would find a way to make it happen. But I knew it was wrong. This wasn't Larry's problem. And after the intensity of last night, there was no way in hell Eamon would forgive the debt.

"I don't think there's anything we *can* do. You know, Dad won't even admit he has a problem and he won't talk to anyone about his addiction."

Not that I'd tried yet. I hadn't. Everything had happened so quickly but seeing as he was forty grand in debt to a mobster, it was safe to say Dad wasn't open to conversations about his addiction. Well that *and* the fact that I'd spent hours researching gambling addiction and the one thing I had learned for sure was that addicts never want to admit they have a problem much less talk about it.

"Pete was always a stubborn old fool. I promise not to butt in too badly, but how about I give him a call or drop in to see him?"

My shoulders relaxed because it felt nice to have backup, even if it was a few years too late. "Thanks. Maybe seeing a familiar face will help."

It probably wouldn't, but dammit, I was desperate.

"It can't hurt."

That was for damn sure. "Thanks, Uncle Larry. Now tell me, how's retirement treating ya?"

He laughed that same roaring laugh I remembered, like he was just a little rusty and was still getting used to how it felt to laugh. "Damn good, little girl, damn good. I get some fishing done, plenty of fishing actually and this place keeps me busy."

It was nice to just sit there and drink a beer with a guy who was basically family at ten in the morning, listening as he told me all about taking up hiking and how he thought he'd hate it, but it turned out Larry liked to spend time alone. "Alicia doesn't mind?"

"Hell no. You see this kitchen? She's learning to cook dishes from all over the world so when I come back, she's got all this food waiting for me to try. And you know what, it all tastes so damn good. And she loves hearing me tell her how much I love her food."

The red flush of his cheeks told me exactly what he was talking about.

"Sounds like an ideal retirement."

"Better than that."

"I'm happy for you." I was. "Would it be all right if I stopped by again?"

I could tell Larry was shocked, but he covered it quickly and flashed a genuine smile. "We'd like that. And I'm sure Alicia'd love to cook for you."

"Sounds like a plan." I pulled out a business card and left it on the table. "Thanks, Uncle Larry."

"No problem, Layla. And hey, don't worry too much about your old man. He won't get better until he wants to and there's nothing you can do about it. That's a fact."

I nodded because yeah, I knew that. Logically. But my poor dumb heart didn't want any part of that logic. No, I wanted to find a way to make my dad stop gambling forever. It was a childish thought. Hell, it was a dream, but I couldn't just do nothing.

"I hear ya," I said half-heartedly.

"Yeah, but do you get what I'm saying? I can tell by looking at you that you don't. That's all right, we'll be here when you need us."

"Thanks."

I had a few more names on my list of friends that had been likely family growing up. But like Larry and Alicia, they hadn't been around for years. Still, I had a feeling they would all tell me the same story. Or some variation of it. I wasn't sure I wanted to hear it, now.

I remembered the poker games in the garage that used to happen every Friday night, but by the time I started waiting tables at an Italian restaurant at sixteen, those games had stopped. Probably because my dad stopped getting a thrill from playing poker with his buddies for a few bucks. It wasn't enough for him.

By the time I parked my car and made my way to the office I had more questions. How bad was my dad's problem, really? Maybe he owed ten more people like Eamon more money? Maybe they would come to me to pay his debt? Or sell me on the street to the highest bidder? Or cut me open and make me carry drugs across the border like the drug mules?

Fuck.

At this point anything was possible.

Chapter Twelve

Eamon

When people thought about the mob, it was always guys in shiny suits threatening people with cement shoes and machine guns. They wanted to see the dark side, the exciting side of a life of crime. Organized crime in particular. They'd be bored out of their fucking skulls following me around while I picked up envelopes of money from other past due debtors.

Unfortunately, most of them were like Wayne Kagan, a dentist with a borderline gambling problem who always pushed his payments as late as possible without suffering physical harm. I showed up at his office looking as threatening as I could in a designer suit tailored perfectly for my body.

"Got something for me, Wayne?"

The man was comfortable in his skin for a guy with a thinning crown and about six inches too short and a belly that looked to be about six months pregnant. He didn't flinch, didn't go pale at my appearance, just gave a sharp nod and turned away. "Come on in, Connelly."

This guy. I wanted him to be late just once to give me a reason to beat the shit out of him, always making us jump through hoops just to get the fucking money he was desperate to borrow in the first place.

"Well?"

Wayne ducked behind a tan waist-high desk with a blue strip across the center. After ruffling around in the desk for nearly a full fucking minute, he found what he was looking for and grinned. "Here we are and there you go." He handed over the envelope with a smile. "Paid in full."

"One of these days, Wayne, I swear I'm gonna enjoy pounding your fucking face in."

The motherfucker laughed. He *laughed.* Like I was some big damn joke. If I were a lesser man, I'd put him down just to prove I could.

"It's not like that Connelly. I have to be discreet in case the wife gets wind of my activities, so I waited until after a few invoices were paid to make sure I had the cash for you. And now I do."

I couldn't argue with that. Goddammit. "See you soon."

"I hope not," he said giddily. "I've been on a hot streak lately. Another reason you had to wait." Another gambling addict superstition, but it wasn't my job to cure them, only to collect the money.

"Let's not do this again." I grumbled.

I didn't wait for a response because I needed to get to Patrick's before he blew a goddamn gasket. Heaven forbid, grown men would show up late to a meeting with no set time. But it was a price we all had to pay for the privilege of learning the business from the master.

We all knew, the same way our father did, that he wouldn't be at the top much longer. Not because he was losing his mind or his influence, but the signs of his illness he tried to hide grew more obvious with each passing day. We all had a lot to learn before that time came, which is why I hauled ass and smiled when I walked inside his office and found out I was the first to arrive.

"Suckers," I mumbled to myself with a satisfied grin, waving to Patrick sitting behind his desk.

"It's about time you got here, son."

"Right on time, I'd say. And I come bearing bills," I told him, holding up all the envelopes of varying colors I'd picked up that morning. Some even handed over envelopes with their business logo right on the front. It was shocking how much personal information people revealed to the people they shouldn't.

"Good. Good. Hand it over."

I did and, as always, Patrick opened each envelope carefully, his hands shaking just a little as he counted every bill and wrote a note in the big ass leather ledger where he kept track of everyone who owed him, owed the family. Money or favors, to Patrick they were one and the same. The green and brown leather book with yellowing pages was filled with his chicken scratch handwriting, years of debts and favors, paid or still waiting for the opportune moment to be repaid.

Finally he shredded the last envelope and swiped all the confetti into the metal mesh trashcan beside his desk and grinned. "Good job, Eamon. I can always count on you."

That was good to hear, I supposed, even if he hadn't named which of us, me, Shae or Rourke, would take over as head of the family.

"Thanks. How are you feeling?"

"I'm fine, son. I can't complain. How is that Michaels situation coming along?"

Ah, that was Patrick, master of deflection.

"Fine. I'll check in with him again tonight, and you have my guarantee the money will be in your hands soon." I knew I'd put the cash up myself because that was how we did business. We either got our money or found another way to make them pay, but this shit wasn't like the movies.

Killing people who owed you money only guaranteed that you wouldn't get paid. We broke body parts and beat the fuck out of people as incentive. But addicts were stubborn fucks, every last one of them, which meant after an ass whooping or two, we had to put them to work to pay off the debt. So I either had to present Peter Michaels to work off his debt or the forty plus grand he owed.

Since I couldn't think about anything other than fucking Layla again, even moments after burying my cock deep inside her tight little cunt, I'd have to pay the cash.

"See that ya do," Patrick said, his deep voice still slightly accented, breaking into my thoughts.

"I already said I had it handled. Shouldn't we be talking about something more pressing, like the goddamn Milano assholes?"

The Milano family was technically part of our ... *network*, in a weird way. We used the Milano family because no one could clean up a scene the way they could. If you wanted someone disappeared, they could make it look like the person just packed up and walked away from their life. If you needed a crime scene rigged, they could find a patsy or make it look like a suicide. They were good at what they did, but lately those assholes thought they were destined for more.

At our expense.

Patrick nodded, his brows crinkled deep in thought. "You have a point but son, you worry too much."

"E-money is always looking for something to worry about," Shae said, wearing a big grin as he strolled in. "Good morning, Da'."

"Morning? It's damn near afternoon and you're late. You too, Rourke."

Looking unruffled as always, Rourke waltzed in wearing jeans, a mint green button up and no tie. How in the hell the guy with the straight role didn't have to dress up all the time was beyond me, but Patrick never said a damn word to him. "Can't be late if you don't set a time, Uncle Patrick."

Rather than lashing out as expected, Patrick's face broke into a grin. "Smart ass."

"Learned from the best."

"Yeah, Fiona was always such a smart ass." They shared a laugh because we all knew Aunt Fiona was the biggest smart ass in the family.

"So, Eamon thinks we ought to worry about the Milanos."

Rourke sighed and I waited for him to agree with Patrick, his default position on all things.

"He's right. I heard about an underground game so I went to check it out. The door was run by Milano muscle and the room had Milano stink all over it. The room was shitty and rundown, dark lights and the tables were stained with what I hoped was booze and not jizz." Rourke shuddered. "The cocktail girls were butt ass ugly but their bodies were on point. The drinks were watered down and the tables were legit with enough edge they surely turned a profit last night. A tidy one judging by the amount of traffic inside."

"Shit. That means they promoted that shit somewhere. How?" I asked. They weren't *in* the gambling game, which meant one thing. "They had help."

"Had to have," Shae said, eyes blazing with fury. "I'll get out on the streets and find out who, so we can make them pay."

Despite his easygoing nature, Shae could be a beast when he felt threatened.

"Motherfuckers think they can take on the Connelly's? They better fucking think again."

"Calm down Shae. We have nothing to worry about but we should keep an eye on them anyway."

Shae nodded, but I could see that glint in his eyes that said he wouldn't let it go. He wanted to crack a few skulls.

"I'll put together a team to keep an eye on them. Rourke can supply me with names," he said, staring at our cousin like he'd done something wrong.

"Sure." He stood, barely concealing a smirk. "Let's get to it. I have actual work to do today."

When they were gone, Patrick turned to me. "There will always be someone trying to edge in on our organization, son. The key is to handle it with a certain level of detachment. If you get worked up like Shae, you will make emotional decisions. This seat here," he motioned to the big chair where he spent most of his time. "This seat is the glue of the family, but the decisions made here are on behalf of the whole Connelly organization not just the Connelly family."

I blinked. "They're not the same thing?"

"Not always, no. The organization, the business must come first and if you find a way to cut down a rival, you fucking take it. For the sake of the business. No matter what."

Patrick's words sank in, playing around in my mind for the rest of the day. Organization first, family second. It ran counter to everything I believed about Patrick's role in the family and I spent the rest of the day trying to retrain my brain to think that way.

If I wanted to lead this family, this *organization*, and I damn well did, I had to think that way. Act that way.

And I would, as soon as my nights with Layla were over.

***

My cock stirred with anticipation as the seven o'clock hour drew near, knowing that Layla would soon show up, wet and primed for me to slide into her hot little body all night long. I just hoped we could bypass all the awkwardness from last night.

And small talk. I fucking loathed small talk. It served no point other than to lubricate social inhibitions frowned upon by the masses. There was nothing wrong with dropping by for the sole purpose of a hard fuck and pretending otherwise was just bullshit. She knew what this was and what it wasn't, so why should we pretend?

At seven on the dot the car pulled up and I smiled. Layla was determined, I'd give her that. That was fine by me because tonight, she wouldn't be going anywhere for a good long while.

"Layla, come in, please."

My lips curled at the way her pulse spiked at my words.

"Eamon."

She walked in, hips swaying in a sexy little black leather dress. It was short, hugged her body like a goddamn glove and showed just enough cleavage to make my mouth water.

"Layla, you look …" I didn't even have the words, not when my gaze caught on her mostly bare back with nothing but a strip across the middle, stopping just before the little dents above her ass. "Hot as fuck."

She turned slowly, and my mouth went dry. "Small talk, Eamon?" Her lips were painted bright pink and shiny, like a beacon drawing my gaze to her. All I could think about was having those bright lips wrapped around my cock. Would it leave streaks of pink so I could relive the moment later or would it stay perfect? Untouched, even.

When Layla reached for one strap and slid it over her shoulder and then the other, my cock strained against my zipper. So damn slowly she slid the dress over her hips and down her legs until it was nothing more than a leather pool at her feet. Then she kicked it over to me. "I thought we were past all that."

I watched her turn, flimsy red silk bra and panties sliding against her skin with every step she took away from me. She was headed for the bedroom and I was hot on her trail. After I entered, she locked the door.

"Feeling bold tonight, Layla?"

She stretched out on the middle of the bed, resting on her elbows so that all I could see was two hard nipples poking through the silk. Eager for my mouth.

"Not bold, no." Her legs rubbed together gently, like she was so turned on that she couldn't stand it. "Is this a problem?"

Not for me, it wasn't. I loved a woman who could fuck without pretense.

"You finally wised up, realized it was hot as fuck between us so who gives a shit how it came to be?"

"Something like that," she confirmed, licking her pink lips. "Are we going to psychoanalyze this or are we going to fuck?"

Fuck. "I like the sound of that. Come here." My fingers curled and beckoned her over.

Layla shook her head, blonde waves tumbling around delicate shoulders, brushing against the bright red silk.

"You don't want to come, Layla?" That hitch in her breath set my heart thumping against my chest. And then she began to move.

Slowly. Sensually. She took her time sliding to the edge of the bed, making every move look sexier than it should. "Oh, I do, Eamon. I want to come."

"That's ah, good." My head fell back and a smile curved up my mouth as her hands slid up my abs and over my chest, taking my shirt along with her until it was a heap on the floor beside us. "Because."

"Because?"

Her tone was playful and I had to see that gleam in her eyes. They were sparkling with lust when I looked at her, watched as she played with my chest, obviously fascinated by the hills and valleys of muscle under her hands.

"Damn you are really ripped."

A deep chuckle erupted from me, something that had never happened when a woman had her hands on me, showing me she was fascinated by the landscape of my body. "You didn't notice before?"

"Yeah but not like this." Her voice was filled with awe as one hand played along my muscles, fingertips grazing over nipples until she pulled a hiss of pleasure from me.

"I can kind of see why you're so cocky," she moaned as her other hand dipped inside my pants and wrapped around my cock.

Her hands were pure torture and I couldn't get enough. She added enough pressure to make me groan again, smiling with satisfaction at every sound she pulled from me.

"Layla."

"Yes?"

I wanted to groan in disappointment when her hand left my chest but she worked quickly until my pants and boxers were at my ankles.

"You wanted to say something?"

Her hand, so soft and so fucking warm, squeezed tighter and another groan escaped, my head fell back again as my eyes closed.

"Fuck, yes." Her lush lips wrapped around my cock and I took a second to savor the feel of her mouth, the slick moisture of her tongue, the soft friction of her lips and the heat of her mouth worked to undo me. I succumbed to the pleasure for several strokes, licking my lips at the way she grabbed my ass cheeks, holding on to me like she planned to eat my cock whole. "Fuck."

It was so good.

Hot and enthusiastic. That was what made good head. It wasn't mechanical, the way she used her tongue along the underside of my shaft and pushed her lips together to maximize friction. Layla was into it, making love to my cock with her mouth like it was all of her favorite comfort foods rolled into one.

She took me deeper and deeper, nails digging indentations in my ass and thighs. And then I was at the back of her throat trying like hell not to flex or fuck her pretty little mouth the way I wanted to. Not yet anyway. Then she did it. She opened her throat and closed around the tip of my dick and moaned.

She motherfucking *moaned.*

And my control snapped. I reached down and grabbed a handful of her hair, holding Layla still, at my mercy for just a second and I slid my cock down her throat. "You want it?"

She nodded, her eyes wide and hungry.

"You fucking want it, Layla?"

She swallowed around my cock and I groaned. She nodded.

My cock went deeper and deeper still until her eyes began to water. "Is it enough?"

In response her tongue slid out and caught the edge of my nuts.

My hips jerked and sent me deeper into the wet heat of her mouth while her tongue swished back and forth over my cock.

"Goddamn, Layla. I can't wait to fill that pretty mouth with my come, but right now I need that pussy."

Heat flared in her eyes when I picked her up and tossed her on the bed, my cock went hard at the way her tits jiggled beneath the sexy lingerie.

"You have a filthy mouth, Eamon." She grinned and slid off her silky bra that kept those nipples hard and kissable.

"You like my dirty mouth, remember?" Before she could answer I put my mouth between her legs, tongue slicking over that swollen, wet pussy through her panties.

"Tell me you like it."

She resisted. Layla liked this game where she pushed me to the edge until I snapped.

"Oh."

That was it, a small moan escaped. She wanted to play.

I pulled away her panties and wrapped my lips around her clit, hard, until she screamed and squirmed beneath me. Wild fingers grasped at my hair as she ground her pussy into me.

"Oh fuck, oh God!"

Those words made me suck her clit harder and harder until I felt the tension in her thighs, her ass, her abs. Until she was seconds from coming.

"What the," she screamed as I got ready. Then, "...oh!"

"Fuck!" I moaned when I slammed my cock deep inside her pussy. It quivered and squeezed around me, her orgasm splashing out in bursts while I pumped into her.

Layla's orgasm was never ending, pulling me deeper and I couldn't stop the pleasure rolling through me. I couldn't stop fucking her. Every thrust brought me closer to an explosion. Her every scream inched us both closer to something hot. Something impossible.

"Ah fuck, Eamon. Yes." She moaned low and deep, legs wrapped tight around me as the last aftershocks of her orgasm hit.

I fucked her hard and fast, so deep she winced even as she begged me for more. I gripped her hips hard and rammed into her to the sounds of her shouting my name until hot lava rushed out of me, between us, creating more friction. Volcanic friction that quickly pulled the orgasm from me.

"Oh fuck, Layla. Shit."

My hips kept moving because they couldn't fucking stop, not as long as she pulsed around me in an orgasm that wouldn't quit. "Fuck!"

Her pussy was addictive. I was drunk on the feel of her tight cunt wrapped around my cock as I slid in and out, wet and hot. I wanted more and even though I still had all night, I knew it wasn't enough.

"Fuck yeah," she panted out. And then she burst out laughing.

Chapter Thirteen

Layla

"Okay, now I really do need to hydrate. You're killin' me."

Eamon was insatiable and not in the way of some twenty-or-thirty-something guys where they jackrabbit into you as many times as you'll let them, not giving one damn about your pleasure. Oh no, Eamon got off on getting me off, which only made me hot and horny trying to get him off. It was a vicious cycle for the past four hours and I enjoyed every goddamn second.

Even as I waited for the other shoe to drop. For the asshole version of Eamon to rear his ugly head and kick me out. Again. Instead he smiled and twirled a finger around a lock of my hair. "You mean I didn't fill you up with enough liquid?"

"Dirty, dirty boy." I didn't know what, but there was something about him that turned me into a giggly little schoolgirl. "As great as you are at filling me up, I'm seconds away from passing out."

"Can't have that, can we?" He ground against me, his cock sliding between my lips deliciously. And then he was gone. All I saw was a naked ass, a fine *naked* ass, as it walked away. Damn, it was a fine ass. So fine I just wanted to bite into it. "Ice cold or room temperature?"

"Yes," I told him gratefully, reaching out for both bottles to soothe my parched throat.

"Feeling thirsty?"

I wiggled my eyebrows. "You know it, babe."

"You shouldn't look so fucking hot when you come. Or sound so dirty when I fuck you from behind and flick your clit."

I shivered at his words or maybe it was the stream of cold water that dripped from my chin down my chest and straight between my boobs. Eamon's eyes focused on that one little drop while I finished the first bottle.

"You make me dirty," I admitted to him.

There was a gleam in his eyes, a sparkling satisfaction that lit up his whole face. "Aww princess, are you trying to make me feel special?"

"Nah. I think your ego is sufficiently stroked all day. Every day."

Not that it wasn't warranted, because it was. Eamon was a fucking god when it came to getting me off. He knew my body better than I did, making me come in ways guaranteed to make me blush, even alone in the shower.

"I got something else you can stroke."

It was childish humor to be sure, but when nine inches of thick, hard cock was at my disposal, what was a girl to do? "Oh yeah, what?"

"This." The thick, blunt tip of his cock was perched between my lips. Not forced inside but not timidly waiting for permission. I opened wider and his hips pushed him deeper.

"Mmmhmm." I moaned.

"Oh, shit. You want to play dirty?" He grabbed my hair again, hard enough that it stung a little at the root. I should have balked or at least smacked his hand away, instead my thighs grew wet and sticky and I closed my eyes and savored the taste, the heaviness of him on my tongue. With every stroke I licked him or took him deeper, drawing the most deeply erotic sounds from him.

Who knew it would feel so good to bring a man to his knees with my mouth? Not that I was a prude, but sex with Eamon was like something out of this world. "Mmm," I moaned around him again, feeling more moisture flood between my thighs as his muscles tightened and his cock twitched in my mouth.

"Fuck. You are such a dirty girl," he grunted, gripping my hair while he slowly fucked my mouth, hips moving faster and faster as pleasure took control of him. I should have felt degraded, but I didn't. I felt powerful. Every swipe of my tongue, every move I made drew another sound from him.

"Fuck, Layla."

And that was just what Eamon did, pounded my mouth and played with my boobs while he took the pleasure I gave him. He went deeper, so deep I thought I might choke on him, but he was strangely gentle considering what he was doing to me.

"Look at me." I did and the sight I saw, stunned me. His gaze was pure melted gold, dark desire written all over his face as he thrust in and out of my mouth, one hand gripping my hair to hold me in place and I'd let him. Submit to him because giving him this kind of pleasure gave it right back to me.

"Yes," he whispered, his voice husky with desire. "Just like that. Such a fuckable little mouth."

I smiled and flattened my tongue under his cock and that was when I learned the meaning of losing control. I saw the moment all civility fled and the primal beast inside of him took over, gripping my hair tighter while he fucked my mouth hard, slamming my throat over and over, growling his pleasure until he froze, went still with the buildup of pleasure until it exploded out of him.

"Ah, fuck!" That roar was worth everything. He held my head tight and his jizz shot out of him like a volcano.

"You like that, don't you, dirty girl?"

I nodded even as I continued to suck him dry, taking every drop of his come simply because I liked the way he jerked each time my tongue swiped the sensitive ring around the head of his cock. My tongue dipped into the slit of his cock.

"Enough!" He grabbed my ankles and spun me around, dropping before me and burying his face between my thighs, making wicked wet noises that might have embarrassed me under normal circumstances. What should have embarrassed me even more was that it took two, maybe three swipes of his tongue before my body coiled tight with tension and sprang free in an orgasm that nearly tore me apart.

"Oh fuck, Eamon. Yes!" I gripped his head and ground against him like the hussy he had turned me into until the last sparks of orgasm left my body.

"I guess you like it when I fuck your mouth."

"I'd say I'm not the only one." My back arched and another moan escaped as he slid his tongue deep inside me, making my hips swirl all on their own.

"The difference is that I can make you come again and again. And you know what, Layla?"

"W-what?" the word barely made it out as the tip of his tongue traced my opening, teasing me until I felt another orgasm building in me.

"I plan to make you come until you tap out."

My body was more than up for the challenge, but one look into his green and gold-flecked eyes, dark with lust and I worried about that flash of something I couldn't decipher when he looked at me like that.

***

"I should probably get going." It was well after midnight and I was completely wrung out. My body hummed with a constant arousal I wasn't sure would ever leave, but I knew I couldn't take Eamon again. Which meant I was no longer useful to him.

"What's your hurry?"

The way he traced a finger up and down my arm, like a genuine lover, made it hard to remember why I was here in the first place. But under his gentle, seductive touch, I'd begun to wonder why I was in a hurry to get back to my empty apartment when I could stay here. I might even remember what it was like to sleep in someone's arms again.

"You got a hot date or something?" he asked.

"In the middle of the night? What kind of girl do you think I am?" I immediately realized my mistake in asking that. "Don't answer that."

Eamon chuckled, the sound deep and rich as he pulled me closer so I could feel that he was ready to take me again.

"I think you had no idea what a freak in the sheets you were until last night. I also think I enjoyed unleashing your inner sex goddess."

He kissed that spot behind my neck that was guaranteed to turn me into a puddle, long and slow and with a lot of tongue.

"And then, I think, if you called me in the middle of the night offering up your sweet cunt, I'd break traffic laws to get to you."

Yeah, that dirty talk really did it for me. Even though I knew I couldn't take anymore, my back arched against him, pussy seeking him out like a missile seeing its target. "Eamon, I can't."

"I know, but I wonder, have you ever come just from having your tits licked?"

I barked out a laugh. "That's an urban myth."

His lips curled up into a darkly seductive grin. "We'll see about that. For now I need food. Come."

Wrapped in his t-shirt that was somehow still warm and smelled of him, I followed Eamon to his kitchen where there was plenty of food warming in his ovens. As in multiple ovens. "Are you having a party?"

"I didn't know what you liked so I had my chef make a few things."

He didn't blush or look ashamed and that was a damn turn-on. It was nice even if it was totally unnecessary. I didn't expect all this, hell I didn't expect a bologna sandwich given our arrangement, but I appreciated it.

"You chose good. And now I'm grateful for all the calories burned."

There was fried chicken, pulled pork, steak and shrimp scampi plus roasted vegetables and mashed potatoes.

"So grateful."

He snorted. "I guess the orgasms don't count?"

I looked up and grinned. "Oh they count. But they were a bonus. You got moves, so even if you hadn't gotten me there, it still would've been fun. The fact that you get me off every time is a bonus. And now with the food, well, that's a double bonus."

Maybe I'd drop a few pounds from this insatiable beast. I piled an ungodly amount of mashed potatoes on my plate, feeling no reason to pretend I needed to be cute and girly for him. Eamon wanted to possess me and while we were in bed, I had no problem with that. As long as I didn't let myself think about it too hard.

"You're thinking way too hard over there, Layla."

I looked up and realized he'd already made himself a plate, two actually, and had sat down to eat.

Joining him, I said, "I was just wondering, how does one become a mobster? Do you call yourselves mobsters? Is it like in the movies, your dad is like the Godfather and you're a made man?"

His lips twitched and I decided it was a damn good thing Eamon was an asshole instead of one of those charming playboys who smiled all the time. That scowl had saved many women from heartache, of that

I was certain, because his smile, even a hint of a smile was devastating.

"Born into it. No. Kind of, basically and pretty much."

"Did you have a choice?" I asked, flicking a napkin onto my lap.

In the movies there was always one son who wanted to go to college and pursue a legitimate career and I wondered if Eamon was so angry because he was that son.

"Yes," he said, digging into his food. "Did you?"

I laughed. "Yeah. My dad didn't even realize what was going on, he was drinking all the time. I paid for the tests and admissions and he never knew until I came to him and said, 'Dad I'm leaving for UCLA on August fifteenth'. Totally stunned."

My dad was proud, but hindsight was twenty-twenty and all that and I realized he was more upset that he would have to fend for himself while I was away at school.

"I could've majored in philosophy," I told him, "and it wouldn't have mattered."

Eamon nodded in recognition. "Yeah, I could've done something else, too, but by the time I realized it, I was in too deep."

"A real troublemaker, huh? I can see that."

"A troublemaker yeah, but with violent tendencies."

His gaze hit me head on so that I could see exactly who he was. I liked knowing, because I was making damn sure his orgasms didn't breach any of the walls I'd put up.

"I enjoyed beating the shit out of people a little too much to become a football coach."

Even though his words were sad, they were also funny and I found myself laughing. Hard. Ridiculously hard that turned mildly unladylike thanks to the piece of fried chicken in my hand. "Sorry, it's just, the imagery."

"Glad to amuse you, princess."

I laughed again, happily digging into more food. "Seriously though, how do you become a mobster and what do you call yourselves?"

His laugh was deep with an echo. A man's laugh. "We call ourselves family because that's what we are."

"Like *the five families*?"

He laughed again and sweet Lord above, I might've been willing to do all manner of kinky shit to hear it again. "No. We're not Italian, we're Irish. My grandfather immigrated when he was a kid. We just take care of the city and keep the bad guys out."

"Aren't you the bad guys?" I asked with a wink.

He sighed. "No, do you think loaning people money to help them out of a bind is a bad thing?"

"Are you satisfied with your work?"

I'd always thought gangsters were either sociopaths or tortured souls searching for a way out. But maybe that was what Hollywood wanted me to think. His answer surprised me.

"Yeah, I am actually. I love what I do."

"Then you're luckier than most."

"Are you?" he asked. "Satisfied with your life?"

I nodded, surprised he even gave a damn to ask. "I am. For now. I like what I do and my boss is cool, but I hope I'm not in this position five years from now."

"What position do you hope to be in?"

How could it be that this fucked up situation was the best date I'd had since coming back to Rocket?

"Leading my own team or maybe even working in my own little boutique marketing shop."

"A girl with dreams."

"Damn straight, buster. I have plans for my career and my life."

"Smart girl."

"Woman," I corrected. "Smart woman."

"Sexy woman," he shot back with that grin that had me crossing my legs. "But a dirty girl."

And just like that, the food, the conversation was forgotten as we both succumbed to our baser urges.

Chapter Fourteen

Eamon

I fell asleep with Layla's curves pressed up against me, her blonde hair draped over my face and my chest, and one leg thrown over mine. It was a rare occasion that I fell asleep with a woman, because I didn't trust anyone outside of my family to watch out for me. And sleeping was when I was most vulnerable.

After dinner was interrupted, with more orgasms for me and three for her, we'd both collapsed and passed out. Waking up with a soft, warm woman beside me was a novelty and I let myself enjoy it for the moment, because it wasn't something I planned to repeat. Ever.

I had to remind myself of that when I turned to face Layla. Her face was so calm and serene in sleep, but even then, I could see the dark circles under her eyes, proof that she wasn't as unaffected as she appeared.

I should have been goddamn grateful that she wasn't making a big production out of her worry or fear for her old man. Hell, I should have been jumping up and down that she'd agreed so easily to my demands and that she took so much fucking pleasure from it. She even seemed to forget the real reason we were together. But when she snuggled closer, it did something to me.

Made me forget about the fucking Milanos who were trying to hone in on Connelly territory and businesses. That was dangerous. Too fucking dangerous. It was why Shae, Rourke and I had always steered clear of anything resembling a relationship with a woman. Hell, with anyone who wasn't family. I'd learned long ago only to trust family; they were the ones who'd have my back when the shit hit the fan. And in our world, the shit *always* hit the fan.

Which meant none of us had the luxury of being able to relax with a woman. To just fucking *be* with a woman.

No, we all knew the deal and we lost ourselves in a sea of nameless, faceless women who fit into the lifestyle we'd chosen. Despite what Layla thought about the organization, Patrick had given us each a choice. Join the family business and one day we'd be at the top, running shit the way we'd seen him do since we were kids, or go to college and attempt to have a normal life and do the bidding of some asshole.

Normal, now, that was a joke. There was no fucking way in hell that we'd ever be comfortable with normal, not with the shit we'd seen.

Layla stirred beside me and I braced myself for her to wake up, to ruin this peaceful moment with mindless chatter women seemed so fond of. But she didn't. Her eyes opened, and her lush mouth curved into a smile, one hand drifting lazily across my chest. Then with a soft moan, her eyes closed and her head lolled on my chest as her hand rested so close to my cock, I was tempted to turn over and slide right into her. Waking her up properly.

"You're doing a lot of thinking for the middle of the night," she purred against my chest.

"Just thinking." About too many damn things to be able to go back to sleep.

Layla's hand stopped the gentle, dizzying stroke of her fingers and she looked up at me. "Do you want me to go?"

I was half tempted to say yes just to see how she would respond. So far Layla had acted exactly the opposite of what I'd expected, which had my thoughts all twisted up. The fact that I wanted her to stay was a red flag that she needed to get the fuck out, but the second she began to move away from me, to remove herself from my arms, I tightened my hold on her.

"You're not going anywhere yet." Yet being the operative word. I didn't keep women around and, in that regard, Layla would be no different.

"Sounds good," she murmured, her voice still thick with sleep as she turned over and pressed her back against my chest. I didn't need any encouragement to turn around and fit my body against hers, one hand full of a soft, plump tit with a semi-hard nipple pressed against my palm. The other hand rested low on her hip, my cock cradled into the warmth of her ass cheeks and my face full of the peach scent of her hair.

Before I could remind myself that this was an anomaly, something that could not or would not happen again, I found my body growing heavy as it was pulled under by exhaustion and satisfaction. And sleep.

Sweet, blessed sleep.

Chapter Fifteen

Layla

The sliver of light peeking through heavy dark curtains sliced right across my eye and pulled me from the warm comfort of a peaceful sleep. Wait, curtains? I didn't have curtains in my apartment and my bed was nowhere near this comfortable. Sitting up quickly, I scanned the room with dark, clearly masculine furnishings. Deep navy blue with touches of gold were everywhere and then I remembered.

Eamon.

Last night with him had been incredible. If the first night had been good, and it had, the second night had been a revelation. Who knew the human body was capable of such endless pleasure? Who knew there were men out there so wholly dedicated to getting a woman off, to making her pleasure his first priority? In my short time on this earth and my brief but mostly unsatisfying encounters with the opposite sex, I would have said not one man on this planet was capable of such a feat. But Eamon had proven me wrong.

Not only was he insatiable and dirty as fuck, but he brought the same out of me. I looked to the side of the bed where the navy blue and gold comforter hung half off the bed and my skin heated up at the memory of the way Eamon fucked my mouth. I would have been scandalized had it been any of my past lovers. But even now, with flashes of it playing in my mind, I wanted to do it again. Giving over that power while still maintaining all of the control was a heady experience, but it was more than that.

The way he'd come undone, the dark look in his eyes as he pumped in and out of my mouth saying the most wickedly nasty things to me made me feel like some kind of sex goddess. The way I ground my pussy against his mouth, begging him to taste more of me, to lap up my juices, was so unlike me, I had to relive the moment to make sure I hadn't dreamed it up.

And I hadn't imagined one iota of last night's encounter. It was all real and replaying in my mind like reruns on Netflix. But the small voice in my mind reminded me that it was morning now. Last night was over and it was time for the walk of shame even though shame was the last thing I felt.

I felt way too many things for a woman who'd had a two-night stand with a gangster who was paying me to fuck him. Talking with Eamon last night had been a mistake. Learning so much about him made him seem human, almost likeable. And goddammit when he flashed his smile, he was as breathtaking as any runway model.

I shouldn't have asked those questions and I definitely shouldn't have remembered the answers or let my fascination with mob movies get the better of me. This wasn't some crazy love story where I'd see through the layers of bad boy to get a glimpse of the good man underneath. There probably wasn't a good man underneath. Even if there was, he wouldn't allow me to see it. To him I was no more than a whore. For a debt that wasn't even mine.

And that was fine. Just fine. Totally fucking fine.

I turned and slid to the edge of the bed where I caught a glimpse of my underwear mingled with his discarded clothes. The silky red panties were a torn, wet mess that I couldn't wear again so I balled them in my hand and picked up the bra that still held indents of the way Eamon had sucked me through the fabric.

God, that man had a mouth made for doing dirty things. Just a flick of his tongue and I was a weak little fool who imagined there was a real man underneath the gangster. But I kept telling myself there wasn't.

If life hadn't taught me that men were not who they appeared to be, recent revelations about my father had. So I straightened my spine and balled the bra up with the panties and slowly crept toward the front door where I was sure I'd find my dress. The house was silent and since the bed beside me had been ice cold when I checked, I assumed Eamon had gotten up and slept elsewhere last night.

I knew I should have gone home.

Sex-only relationships did not include sleepovers and especially not when this wasn't even a sex-only relationship but a transactional one. I spotted my dress near the door and tiptoed over to it, hoping to avoid waking Eamon if he wasn't already awake taking care of mob business.

"Going somewhere?"

His deep voice scared the fuck out of me. I yelped and turned with a glare. "Why are you sneaking around your own house?"

Eamon leaned against the wall looking as good this morning in black silk pajama pants and black tank that showed off miles of muscle and the ink on his arms as he had last night in nothing at all. Only now, he also wore the smug smirk of a man who knew he'd put it down last night. All night.

"The better question is why you're sneaking around my house. Isn't it?"

Feeling defensive and naked because I hadn't quite made it to my dress yet, I crossed my arms.

"I wasn't sneaking, I was trying to leave without disturbing you." And if I was being honest with myself, avoiding a repeat of the previous night's farewell.

"I've been awake for a few hours."

No doubt because there was a stranger asleep in his bed.

"I should've gone home last night," I said.

That one sentence settled in my gut like a lead brick. I *should* have gone home last night so he could go to sleep in his bed. I *should* have gone home last night to keep my head clear.

"I wanted you here."

And I took that to mean that now he wanted me gone.

With a nod, I inched toward the dress, feeling more and more naked the longer his gaze caressed my now overheated skin.

"Okay, well," I said awkwardly. "I should be ..."

"Come on," he said, waving toward the kitchen. "I made breakfast."

"Uhm, what? More food? You know I wasn't angling for an invite."

He smirked but it wasn't that smug smirk that had the ability to make me feel about two inches tall. No this was an amused crinkle around his eyes. "I know that. And you need to eat. Stay healthy."

Without another word, Eamon pushed off the wall and turned to give me a glorious view of his silk covered ass and wide, muscular back. The back of a man, solid and strong. Capable. The narrow waist revealed that he wasn't just in shape, but damn good shape and though they were covered now by silk pants, I knew those legs were powerfully lean. His body was as lethal as any gun, a fact I'd seen up close and personal.

I looked over at the dress still on the floor where I'd kicked it aside and then over at the empty wall where Eamon had been leaning. Staying for breakfast was dumb. It was something a girl did who was expecting more. One-nighters didn't cook breakfast, they didn't even take you out for breakfast afterwards, that wasn't the nature of a one-night stand. Staying would cause more trouble than I was prepared to deal with at the moment.

Then my stomach growled and decided for me.

"Food's getting cold!" he said.

I doubled back to the bedroom, grabbed the discarded t-shirt on top of his jeans and slipped it over my shoulders, grateful it was no longer covered in the warmth of his body because the scent was overwhelming. Leather and sandalwood with a hint of badass and maybe even a little gun residue, whatever that smelled like, for an aroma that was unmistakably Eamon.

"Smells good in here," I said when I arrived in the kitchen. And it did. The scent of coffee hit me first but there was also bacon, and cheese potatoes, and a beautiful fruit salad on the table.

"I hope you're hungry." He said the words without turning around, which I appreciated.

"Kinda, we never finished eating last night. Got too busy fuckin'. Gotta keep up my girlish figure anyway, ya know?" I smiled.

I tried to eat healthy and attend a yoga or aerobics class when I felt up to it. I'd accepted my curves a long time ago and knew wanting something different was pointless. There were enough problems in my life trying to take me down, I didn't want to add my appearance to the pot.

"Your figure seems to be all right to me."

Eamon wasn't a man who uttered meaningless compliments, which made the compliment all the more meaningful. "Thanks, but I wasn't fishing for a compliment."

"Good because I wasn't giving you a compliment to make you feel better. Just stating a fact."

Right. "Okay then. Thanks." He nodded a little and I dug into the frittata that overflowed with bacon and potatoes. "This is good, thank you. Why didn't you just heat up the leftovers from last night?"

His gaze seared through me with the efficiency of a laser beam, surprise warring with something else, suspicion maybe? And it was that last one that reminded me of where I was, who I was with and why.

"Didn't want to and you're welcome," he said with a seriousness I couldn't fathom.

We ate, maintaining the world's most awkward silence, which only made me eat faster. Like a pig at a trough, I shoveled the food into my mouth until my plate was empty. I may not have been the smartest chick in the world, but I could take a hint.

"That was delicious, thank you. Want some help cleaning up?"

I didn't want to stay, but it was the least I could do, after the amazing breakfast he'd made. It was much better than the toasted bagel with peanut butter I usually had for breakfast.

"I have people who take care of that, Layla."

There he was, the smug asshole Eamon who would make it easier to leave.

"Right. Of course. Okay, then. Bye."

This time I practically ran from the kitchen, stopping only to grab my shoes from the bedroom and quickly dressing one foot from his front door. With my underwear balled up in my purse, I felt more like a streetwalker than I ever had in my entire life.

"The limo is waiting for you out front."

I looked up in search of the man who belonged to the voice but he was already gone, vanished into the depths of the house. I shouldn't have been surprised and once I thought about it, I wasn't surprised. Eamon was an asshole who did whatever he wanted, no matter who got hurt. A few well-spoken words and good food wouldn't change that.

KB Winters

Chapter Sixteen

Eamon

"What do you think, E-money?"

Shae turned to me expectantly. We were on site, checking out the newest location for another underground casino. He leaned in, waiting for my opinion.

"Pretty fucking great, right?"

He flashed his wide, toothy smile and looked around, gesturing at the fixtures as if I couldn't see everything right before our eyes.

It was a familiar look. I knew it well and when I looked at the spacious location, I felt it too. The burgundy carpeting with the gold pattern swirling through it was outdated but it had that retro seventies feel I knew our clients would appreciate.

I'd gone over it carefully, did some numbers in my head and said, "It has to be gutted and it'll take about six weeks of work but I think it'll do."

"It'll do? That's all you have to say about this amazing space?" Shae shook his head. "You're getting old if the thrill of the find is gone, brother."

Maybe he was right, I thought. But then, I said, "Maybe you're just overly excited because you found this property."

I had to agree, it was a damn good location and a gem of a find considering how many of these places the Connelly family already operated within Rocket city limits, not to mention the surrounding areas.

"Maybe I am," Shae replied, "but that doesn't mean it's not incredible."

I cast my eyes over at the realtor listening in at us. I scowled at Shae.

"Maybe you should talk a little louder about how incredible it is, so the realtor can jack up the price or even better, start a bidding war for this space."

It was the one thing Shae lacked, good business sense. Maybe it was because he was such a good time guy, working, well, schmoozing the other organizations to keep anyone's feathers from getting a bit too ruffled in this line of work. Or maybe it was because he was the baby of the family. Either way, it was a gap in his education that none of us had been able to fill.

Shae grinned and then shrugged like it was no big deal. "She knows who we are and what we do. No way in hell would she dare." And that was the other problem with Shae. He saw a problem and immediately grabbed the sledgehammer when a scalpel would get the job done.

"This is business baby brother, and we all play the game. Sit back and watch." I strolled over to the realtor with a jovial grin. "Josie, this place looks great, but I think it needs some work."

She flashed a mile wide grin and looked around with an appraising eye.

"The work is all surface, just beauty work and it'll turn into a spectacular place."

"Those bathrooms are more than a beauty job. We'll have to gut them and start over, check the plumbing, too. Maybe even pull up the carpets to be sure there's no mold. You have a report on this place?"

Josie's shoulders sagged in disappointment. "Yeah, I'm sending it to your phone now," she said as her fingers flew over her phone's screen.

"Everything looks good Mr. Connelly and the price is fair with very little wiggle room."

"How little?"

"Ten, fifteen off, tops."

I could work with that. "And what about the parking lot? If you throw that in, I'll pay full price before I even open up the report."

Josie nibbled her bottom lip and just like that, I was transported to this morning with Layla. The way she nibbled her lip when she was nervous or when she was thick in the middle of passion, completely undid me. I couldn't stop thinking about her, dammit. Every fucking thing I saw made me think of her. I imagined laying her out on the bar with the leather bumper, legs splayed wide with my cock buried deep in her sweet pussy.

"Are you even listening?" Shae looked at me like I was a stranger.

"What? Just making plans in my head," I told him casually before turning back to Josie.

"I'll take this to the seller but I can say with confidence we have a tentative deal." She stuck her arm out with a satisfied smile, giving me a firm shake I appreciated. Josie dressed the part of a sexpot but she'd never once attempted to cross the line, which was why we'd made her a very rich woman once she learned how big a premium we put on discretion.

"Sounds good. Let me know when you have a definite answer."

"Will do." She grabbed her bag, stuffed a few papers inside and headed for the door. "Thanks again, Eamon. Shae."

When she was gone, my brother turned to me. "What the fuck, man? You spacing out on business now?"

"What? You're fucking crazy, baby brother. Didn't I just turn your incredible space into a done deal? Get off my ass."

"What's up with you or should I say who? You haven't been yourself lately."

I laughed and shoved my hands in my pocket, taking another long look at the space. "Finally decided to pursue that psych degree so you can move past arm chair psychologist?"

"Don't be an asshole, man. Just tell me that whatever it is won't affect the business."

That pulled a sharp, bitter laugh from me. "That's rich coming from you, Shae."

"Yeah, I know the signs."

I clapped him on the back. "You worry too much. I'm fine and things are fine. I can't help it that I have a lot of shit going on and didn't give you enough attention. Think of it this way, at least I got us parking space out of the deal."

His gaze narrowed in my direction. "The old man will love you more for it."

"Nah, you can take the credit. It means more to you."

"Fuck you, asshole."

"Not my time, brother. And I'm pretty sure that's against the law."

"Not that it ever stopped us before," he added with a smirk. "You did good with the negotiating."

Of course I did, I'd been trained to do this shit since I was old enough to understand the art of negotiation. "You'll learn baby brother, because you're going to secure the vendors to get this place up and running."

"You already cleared it with Dad?"

"No, but I will. Don't worry."

"Hey, you think we should ask Josie if anyone else has come looking for a space similar to this one?"

I smiled at my brother and wrapped an arm around him because I knew he hated it. "That is a great fucking idea, man. Track her down and let me know what you find out."

If we could fuck with the Milanos in any way, make them see how difficult life would be with us as enemies, maybe we could squash this small problem before it became a bigger, deadlier problem.

"On it. Talk soon, E-dogg." Shae hurried toward the door, eager to catch up with the pretty lawyer and find his way into Patrick's good graces, which wasn't necessary but Shae was the only one who didn't believe it.

"My phone is always on." I pulled the phone from my pocket and glanced down at the screen with a smile. I only had two more nights with Layla and after last night, and this morning, I knew it wouldn't be enough to get her out of my system. She was a rare kind of fuck, the kind that fucks with your head and makes you question which way was up. I sent a message.

See you soon, princess.

There, that should keep her on edge. Hot and bothered and curious about what I would do to her next.

I tried to shove aside thoughts of Layla as I went on with the rest of my day, but it was useless. The peach scones served at Patrick's place reminded me of the smell of her hair, the fresh raspberries brought to mind her stiff nipples, hard and aching from my mouth. Everything brought her to mind, so much so that after updating my father on the day's business, I left in a hurry.

Eager for another taste.

Chapter Seventeen

Layla

As if this day wasn't long and busy enough, spending the night at Eamon's meant I didn't have time to pack a lunch. I had to venture out into the cloudy, almost rainy day to get something to eat.

"You sure I can't get you anything, Ross?" I'd been too distracted by Eamon's cryptic text to order lunch until it was too late.

"Nope. My woman's bringing me lunch."

I cut a gaze over at my boss while I packed up my purse and arched a brow. "Is that what the kids are calling it these days?"

"Fingers crossed." With a wiggle of his brows, Ross left my office. Whistling.

Now Ross and Mary? They were a #goals couple. Not only had they been together for more than a decade, but they still went at it like horny college kids, including frequent, fancy date nights.

It was hard not to be bitchy, and I probably would have been if they weren't the nicest, most generous people I'd ever met. Sure, I had every reason to be jealous since I hadn't had a boyfriend since junior year of college. The last date I'd been on was at least four months ago. Maybe six. But I wasn't bothered by what they had. I envied them because I was one of those self-obsessed under thirty's who worried I wouldn't find *the one*. If I envied them at all, it was because of the trust it must take to love someone like that.

Not sure I had that in me.

I grabbed my umbrella and took the elevator down to the lobby, heading toward the deli. I hoped it wouldn't be so packed that I'd spend my entire lunch hour standing in line. At least the rain had stopped; that was the one small saving grace in this hellish day.

I'd arrived at the office early and played catch up for the rest of the morning. Two clients had shown up unannounced to 'see what we had so far,' which was code for they wanted to peek over our shoulders—my shoulder—to make sure we didn't fuck their image up. That hour-long handholding session screwed up my entire morning. As a result, I missed a conference call with a new client and had to move a meeting with my team to after lunch, which meant they would all be sleepy and lethargic instead of upbeat and creative. Hooray for me.

Thank God for lunch breaks.

The sight of a familiar black limo brought me up short. My breath hitched, and my heartbeat ratcheted up double time and then my brain kicked in. Of course it had to be a different limo belonging to some random rich douchebag or one of those couples who thought a quickie wedding in Rocket was the height of romance. Not *him*. Shaking off the elevated heart rate, I tamped down the disappointment and kept walking.

"It's *soon*, princess."

I froze at that deep, seductive voice. It *was* Eamon, damn him.

"What are you doing here?"

"Get in." Without another word the window slid back up and the door opened. Eamon stepped out looking panty melting hot in a dark gray suit.

My feet carried me toward all that male deliciousness, but my mouth never made things all that easy.

"You said four *nights*." My own body betrayed me as the words came out, standing up as if to say, "Shut up bitch, we want this."

"I did," he damn near whispered in my ear as his hands went to my waist and guided me into the limo. "But then something funny happened today. I couldn't stop thinking about you. Hearing you." He inhaled. "Smelling you."

My legs trembled and I was grateful the seat was there to catch me because holy fuck sticks, this guy was potent.

"Sounds like a personal problem."

I wish I wasn't flattered by his empty words but dammit, I was weak.

Eamon slid in and closed the door, pressed a button to lift the privacy window until we were completely alone, nothing but an ovary-exploding smile between us. "It is personal. Very. That's why I'm here because only a personal solution will do."

One hand dropped down to my thigh, gripping it just tight enough that I knew who was in control and then his mouth crashed down onto mine. His mouth took possession of me, sliding across the seam of my lips back and forth, back and forth until I was practically in his lap.

"See, I knew you'd understand."

He smiled and I was thankful that I was already sitting down, because, holy hell, this man should come with an explicit warning labels.

My panties soaked instantly even as my heart pounded in my ears or maybe that was the sound of my blood, thick and hot, rushing through my body. Either way, one hot kiss and one nuclear smile and I was a gone little hussy. A low moan escaped and Eamon swallowed it as his free hand, the one not cupping the back of my head, slid up my thigh until his thumb brushed against my clit.

"Fuck, the sounds you make. Layla."

The way he groaned my name was like a hot steamy night full of want and need, the kind of sticky, sweaty sex that a woman never forgot.

"I need a taste. Now."

He tossed off his jacket, leaving him in a sexy little suit vest that I couldn't look away from, not even as he knelt in front of me and spread my legs apart. I gasped and he smiled a wicked grin, probably straight from the devil himself.

"But..." I didn't want to finish that sentence, because I realized I didn't care that I'd been running around all morning like a crazy person. And my fucking bra and grandma panties didn't even match.

"That's okay Layla, I don't mind." And then his face was buried between my legs, licking and sucking me while two thick fingers invaded my opening, thrusting in and out while his mouth did wet, wicked things to my clit. It was too much, but like the sex junkie I was turning out to be, I couldn't stop. Hell, I probably couldn't under the threat of bodily harm, because the way he tasted me, *really* tasted me, like I was truly his favorite snack, was more addictive than dark chocolate.

Before I could finish my thought, Eamon yanked a powerful orgasm out of me that shook me to my core, vibrating my body while the limo moved smoothly through traffic and the sounds of pedestrians and midday life filtered into our little bubble.

The pleasure went on and on because Eamon, the torturer, wouldn't let it go. His tongue traced my opening again and again, ensuring that my sensitive nerves never got a break, flicking his tongue inside every once in a while just to make my body jerk in response.

"Okay. Okay."

His deep chuckle filled the limo and vibrated my inner thighs.

"Enough?"

"Yes. No." The words came out choppy around my big goofy grin.

"Good answer."

His seductive gaze never left mine as one hand made quick work of his pants and boxers while the other worked to make sure I didn't forget his touch. With that beautiful cock exposed, hard and long, thick and jutting out where I wanted him most.

"Now, I want you to ride me. Make me come, Layla."

Words to my ears. He grabbed me by the waist and lifted me onto his lap, groaning when I slid my pussy up and down the length of his cock. My clit was so swollen that every pass sent a lightning bolt behind my eyes, tingles of awareness zapped through me and skittered across my overheated skin.

"Yes!" I moaned.

"Fuck!" I gripped him tight and lined our bodies up, basically impaling myself on his massive cock and tightened immediately. This position with a guy like him was uncomfortable. Deliciously, wickedly uncomfortable. I couldn't stop moving, my body wouldn't allow it, not with this gorgeous cock throbbing inside of me.

"Layla," he pleaded. With his jaws clenched in restraint, Eamon threw his head back and swallowed another moan.

Watching him in the grip of lust like this did something to me. I leaned forward and scraped my teeth along his throat as I rode him, hard and fast, a woman possessed until we both flew apart.

At.

The.

Same.

Fucking.

Time.

I was pretty sure my body floated away from me and I watched us on a cloud of pleasure. Intense fucking pleasure that caused me to wear a ridiculous grin on my face.

"Damn girl, that was intense," he said, his head lying back on the soft, buttery leather.

It was. Too intense, emotionally and physically. I needed space. Now. Adjusting my panties, which I knew would have to be trashed as soon as I got to a bathroom, I smoothed my skirt, my top and my hair until I looked like any other worker bee rushing around on her lunch break. Except unlike most of the worker bees, my legs were wobbly, my Grammy panties were ruined, and my stomach was empty.

"That was ... amazing as always."

"Honestly," he chuckled, "I like it."

I'm sure the ego stroke didn't hurt one bit. "I aim to please."

"You did, princess. I am whatever the word is just above pleased. I am fucking satisfied, babe."

There went that damn smile again, the one that would replay in my head while my body remembered every moment of today's encounter.

"Now you have something to think about the rest of the day."

"I'll probably be thinking about what I want to eat for dinner for the rest of the day but I'll be sure to pencil you in for a few thoughts as well."

"No need, Layla, because I'm all you'll be thinking about."

He opened a small black door that turned out to be a fridge and pulled out a red and white checkerboard bag. "Lunch."

I groaned. "Pastrami? Now I will be thinking about you all day. A guy who brings me pastrami can't be all bad."

"Sandwich, chips and a thick pickle. Just for you."

I flashed a sickly sweet smile. "I love a thick pickle." I really wanted to ask how in the hell he knew about my love of pastrami, but I was afraid I didn't want to know the answer. "Thanks Eamon, you're a unique lunch date."

He chuckled and opened the door for me, grabbing my ass as he helped me out of the limo. "Just wait until you see what I have planned for dinner."

I couldn't wait and I gave him a wink before turning away, closing the door and striding back into the five-story building that housed my office with an extra *oomph* in my step.

***

I should have known the minute Eamon showed up at my office and gave me an unforgettable orgasm or two, that my day would only go to shit from there. It was inevitable, really and I was more pissed off at myself because I knew better. Good things didn't happen like that, at least not in my life.

The day I won the fourth-grade spelling bee, I ran through the hospital to share the news with my mom, who'd practiced every word with me even from her hospital bed. She'd been so damn proud of me, bragging to all the nurses and doctors about her pretty little genius. It had been a really great afternoon, until just a few hours later when the cancer took her.

So I should have known those orgasms would cost me. But I was too high on them, on Eamon's mouth, his capable fingers and especially his thick cock, to realize that all the pleasure would come at a cost.

It started with the goddamn copy machine which had decided to crap out at exactly two fifteen in the afternoon, exactly forty-five minutes before the New Style people showed up to see what their team had come up with.

Thankfully it wasn't my team, but that hadn't stopped Jamie-Lyn, another account executive, from throwing me under the bus because I'd been printing out budgets for my team when it happened. I could handle being thrown under the bus, if it would save a client. And only then.

"She's trying to sabotage me!" That whiny ass cry made me want to bitch slap Jamie-Lyn, but that would have been a surefire ticket to the unemployment line.

Instead I snorted and rolled my eyes, showing Ross and Brenda the HR lady how ridiculous I thought this whole thing was. "You don't register on my radar enough for me to attempt sabotage, Jamie." Even if I didn't have a gambling addict father who owed a shit ton of money to the mob that I had to actually sell my ass to pay off, Jamie-Lyn wasn't important enough as far as I was concerned.

She sucked in a breath and turned her red-rimmed eyes on me. "You were using the printer when you knew we had an important meeting today."

Ross remained impassive at the table and Brenda wrote notes but her gaze never left us. I sighed again, seriously contemplating a quick throat punch in lieu of a letter of resignation but that kind of reckless behavior was saved for my dad. "Maybe you shouldn't have waited until the last minute to print off what you needed for a client meeting. And for the record, I don't care enough about you to know when you have meetings, Jamie-Lyn!"

Ross' lips twitched at my outburst, but he was a professional and kept it contained, which was smart since the waterworks started in earnest.

"That's not...that's not even close to true!"

This shit was getting ridiculous, I folded my arms over my chest and turned to Ross and Brenda. "Are we seriously considering that I did this, my job, on purpose just to screw with her? Because forty-five minutes before my team meets with a client, we're practicing our pitch. Just saying."

Jamie-Lyn sucked in a breath and I prepared myself for more tears, hysterics, whatever. The glow had long faded on my lunch time nookie and I was just pissed. "She broke the machine!"

"Enough." Ross was quickly losing patience and I braced myself for his outburst. "Layla get back to work."

That was all I needed to hear, letting my four-inch black stilettos carry me back to my office just in time to hand out budget print-outs to my team. "Make sure your numbers come in under the ones highlighted for each department and we won't have any problems. Got it?"

My team was all smiles, but I could see the worry in their eyes and Kade, my resident computer maestro, was the one to voice the collective concern. "You're not in trouble are you?"

More trouble than they knew but that wasn't their concern. "Not that I know of but if you guys hear anything, let me know."

I gave a smile and a quick wink before dismissing them all to get a bit more work done before the day ended in an hour.

"Commit those numbers to heart!"

By the time the workday was officially over, I was exhausted and pissed off and ready for another round of Eamon's fingertips. And to top it all off, I needed to go see my dad, something I had no desire to do while I was using my body to pay off his debts. But he was my dad and the only family I had left in this world, which meant the apartment we'd moved into two years after mom's death was my after work destination.

"Hey Dad, I figured it was—" the words died on my lips at the sight of him asleep in his favorite lounger. Head leaning back with his mouth slightly parted, he looked every inch the middle-aged widower with a gambling problem he was. Asleep though, the wrinkles faded away and he looked like the man I'd known my entire life, not the stranger I realized he'd been for years.

With Dad asleep, I wouldn't get any answers from him. Not that I thought I'd get them if he were awake, but at least then I had a shot. I decided to clean up the place the way I had for most of my life. Looking around the kitchen at the dishes piled in the sink, the multitude of cups littering the countertops, and the six-seater pine table in the corner, I could see how easy it was to be clueless.

Dad had been a good provider, but he wasn't the best housekeeper, which meant chores like washing dishes, making sure the bathrooms were clean and the laundry was done had always fallen to me. And I was happy to do it, along with anything else I could to ease the sadness I saw every time I looked at him. But that meant I missed clues about his drinking and gambling that I shouldn't have.

All the final notice stamps on utility bills, the late nights I never thought about because as a kid I couldn't wait until I was a grownup who could stay out as late as I wanted and the slow trickle of new friends.

Damn! It was all right there before my blind eyes!

And now, like the good daughter I was, I was paying the price.

I finished the dishes and moved to the three stacks of mail on the kitchen table. After sifting through at least two dozen envelopes with late notices, I found something I thought might be able to give me some answers. A bank statement. Twelve hundred bucks and two cents was all the money he had in this particular account, which wasn't too alarming, except that it kind of was.

Not satisfied with just one statement, I went through all the envelopes and set aside the bills that needed to be paid while throwing out all the duplicates. I found two more bank statements and my face went pale as all the blood ran out of it. One account had a bit more cash in it, ten thousand bucks, which pissed me off.

"I'm going to kill you, old man."

He had ten grand just sitting in one account while I was fucking a mobster to keep him from doing God knows what to him!

The other bank statement was a loan statement. A loan for half a million bucks.

"What?"

As soon as I saw that number and the regular payments that were made, I stopped giving a damn about whether or not Dad's precious sleep was interrupted.

Up on my feet, I went to my old room that had since been converted into a junk storage room and exactly where I knew he kept everything I needed to see.

It was all there, boxes and boxes of papers. Nothing was labeled, because in true Peter Michaels fashion, he planned to ignore it all until the problem grew so big that it couldn't be ignored. Bank statements going back five, six years stuck out of every box.

I could see this wasn't the first loan he'd had which only brought up more questions. How did he get these loans and where in the hell did the money go? Did he have cash someplace to actually pay the Connelly's off?

"Dad, wake up!" I yelled for him before I even made it back to the living room.

"Dad! Dad!"

He didn't even stir, and I ignored the flash of worry that maybe he wasn't sleeping, because of course he hadn't just taken a nap in the middle of the day. He was passed out drunk.

"Dad!"

Startled, his eyes opened, hazy and unfocused before he blinked, and a slow smile appeared.

"Hey princess, what are you doing here?"

"I came to check on you Dad and guess what I found? Go on, guess."

I was so furious I could have throttled him the way Eamon had the day we met, but I didn't.

"I found bank statements. From more than one bank and good news Dad, you're rich."

At least he had the decency to look ashamed.

"It's not what you think, honey. I swear it isn't."

He sighed and pushed the footrest down so his feet were planted firm on the ground. "Those loans, that money, it isn't mine."

"Explain."

He didn't want to. I could tell by the defiant lift of his chin and the way he sat just a little taller.

"It's nothing for you to concern yourself with."

"Bullshit. You want to know what I'm doing to pay off *your* debt? Do you Dad?"

He shook his head and snorted.

"Yeah, that's what I thought. Tell me why, according to the bank, you have hundreds of thousands of dollars from several banks right here in town?"

"Casinos and underground gaming rooms need cash. When I couldn't pay the last few times, I took out loans for Connelly, the old man, not Eamon. They pay the loans back on time, and I don't know why they do it this way, only that they do."

"And you couldn't do that this time?"

He shook his head, disappointment radiating off of him in waves.

"Too much already, bank wouldn't approve another until some of these are paid off."

I stared at the man who'd raised me, the man who was supposed to love and protect me and shook my head. I had no words for what I felt. I took a deep breath and nodded. I needed to get out of this place. Away from Dad, away from my thoughts and away from Eamon Connelly.

"I have to go."

"I'm sorry, Layla. Forgive me."

I froze at his words and turned back to my father whose entire body had been swamped by fear. The anguish in his eyes was real and I knew he was hurting inside and that hurt me. But I also knew that a quick mention of some action and his guilt would blow out the door with me.

"I'll do what I can, Daddy."

"That's all I can ask."

I slammed the door behind me, dammit. Angry that he was making me feel sorry for him when I was the one selling my ass to a fucking gangster.

Albeit, a gangster who was a magician when it came to giving a woman pleasure.

Chapter Eighteen

Eamon

I paced in my kitchen, my phone on speaker, listening to my cousin give me an update.

"You really think we have to worry about those Milano assholes?"

I couldn't believe they'd put on an underground game that rivaled ours. We had the hottest chicks Rocket had to offer, stole a few from Vegas, San Francisco and even plenty of the Hollywood and Porn Valley castoffs.

Rourke sighed, the sound filled with tension and frustration. "Hell no, we don't have to *worry*, Eamon, but it's not a bad idea to keep an eye on them. Watch their moves."

And that was classic Rourke, a fucking champion chess player who saw ten moves ahead of everyone else.

"Plus those fuckers can't be trusted and I want to be prepared this time."

I knew exactly what he meant. A few years before Rourke's father was killed in jail, he'd crossed the Milanos and his mother, Aunt Fiona, was the one who'd paid the price.

"Anything you need, man, just say the word."

"Thanks, man."

That was it. A simple word of gratitude and my cousin Rourke was ready to move on.

"Shae can't stop talking about that space he found, but I know that parking lot addition was all you."

I laughed. "Baby brother needs a win and it's no skin off my back to give it to him."

"Nice of you, but damn he's annoying."

We shared a laugh over just how ridiculous Shae could be. As the classic youngest child, he was a goofball and a jokester. Make no mistake, he took his work for the family seriously but that was about it.

"Uncle is happy though."

"And that's why we do this."

A beep sounded to let me know I had a visitor, which was odd since I didn't do business at my house and I wasn't expecting company.

"Hang on Rourke, someone's here."

The silence between us changed. Charged the way it did when you lived a life like ours.

"Expecting company?"

"No."

I was on alert, watching the surveillance cameras that covered the house and the surrounding land and seeing nothing.

"I'll send some men."

"No! Not necessary."

"How can you be sure? Don't be a fucking hero, Eamon."

There on my doorstep was a beautiful blonde vision looking like a sexy librarian in a skintight skirt and a blouse that perfectly outlined her tits.

"Not being a hero, Rourke. The company is female."

Rourke scoffed. "And females are safe? How'd she find you?" His sarcasm wasn't lost on me, mostly because it was no secret that Rourke didn't get serious about women. Ever. He gave them a night, maybe two and then he moved on. Names and faces forgotten.

"Nope. But this particular female is known. And welcome." His deep chuckle sounded in my ear as I made my way to the front door, feeling happy as fuck I'd sent my staff home for the day so I could work.

"Then I'll leave you to it."

"Let me know if you run into another Milano game."

I was eager to see what those motherfuckers came up with, how much they'd stolen from us.

"Worried about me, cuz?"

I barked out a laugh. "I want in on the fucking action when you finally snap." The last thing I heard was Rourke's laugh, loud and amused as the call ended. I pulled open the front door as I slid the phone in my back pocket. "Couldn't wait until tonight?"

Layla glared at me, green eyes so dark they were damn near black but all I could focus on was the way her tits rose and fell under her blouse. She was breathing hard; her skin was flushed and the fire burning in her eyes threatened to burn down the house.

"You forgot to mention that it was only forty grand Dad owed you *this time*, Eamon."

Ah, she was angry, which meant she wanted to do the thing I hated most. Talk.

"Do any of the other times matter, Layla?"

"You know they do!" She got in my face and thought better of it, taking two steps back but I wouldn't allow it, I got right in her face right back.

"Why didn't you say anything?"

"Wasn't my place to say, princess."

"Bullshit. You just didn't want to talk about it."

"Why would I? Those debts have been satisfied, which means they are none of your concern."

I didn't talk family business with women. Ever. And I never would.

"It's my concern if you think you can fuck me to pay off the rest of my father's debts!"

I arched a brow at her acidic words. "Not having a good time, princess?"

"That's not the point!"

"Seems to me it's the only point. At least the only one I'm willing to talk about. Your father is an adult and he knows what he signed up for. If you have questions, then you should probably ask him."

Her little fists moved from her sides up under her tits as she crossed her arms and glared at me.

"I'm asking you." Her face was determined, just like the set of her shoulders, and her tapping foot.

"Then you're asking the wrong person."

The space between us shrank until we were face to face, her angry and me horny as fuck.

"Any other questions or do you want me to make you scream?"

With a self-satisfied grin on her face, Layla looked at me, opened her mouth and then she screamed. It was loud and primal, almost a horror movie scream. As quickly as the scream started it was over.

"Happy?" She asked.

"Not what I had in mind but if it got you sorted, I'm happy. Did it?"

The last thing I wanted was for my uncomplicated sex to become another complication.

"No, dammit! Why won't you answer my questions?"

I took a step forward and blocked her attempt to leave, placing both hands on either side of her head. "I won't answer, Layla, because it is none of your fucking business."

She gasped and pushed at my chest. "Right, I forgot."

She kept pushing until I relented and moved.

"Silly me. I'm out of here!"

Goddammit this was exactly why I didn't deal with women outside the bedroom. Too fucking emotional. Too irrational. "I expect you back here tonight," I called after her and my words were met with an erect middle finger that made me laugh.

Layla was what Patrick would call a firecracker and even that little exchange got my dick hard and aching, throbbing to slid into her wet goodness again. Tonight would come soon enough and if Layla thought she could skip tonight because she was upset, then we'd pick up where we left off tomorrow.

I was a fucking Connelly and I always got what I wanted.

One way or another.

Chapter Nineteen

Layla

I was angry and out of sorts because both Dad and Eamon were doing a damn good job of playing two idiots. I needed to disconnect for a while, to get away from everyone and everything in my life so I turned off my phone right outside of Eamon's place and I drove.

At first I just drove around the streets of Rocket, gazing at the peaks of the Sierra Nevada in the distance. Usually, I barely glanced at the majestic mountains when my gaze landed on them in one of my mirrors but today, I took in the details. The sharp points and steep dips between the beasts, the snowcapped tips. The range was more beautiful than I ever gave it credit for and it was just the kind of scenery I needed to soothe my racing mind.

Dad was in debt. Major fucking debt and it was all the fault of the Connelly mobsters. Okay yeah, Dad bore some responsibility, too, but dammit he had a problem and they were predators, preying on weaker animals and taking what they could before discarding the carcass. But that wasn't even what had my foot pressing down on the gas. It was the fact that I'd used my body to pay off his debt and it likely wouldn't be the last time he racked up tens of thousands of dollars worth of gambling debts.

What would I do then? Definitely not what I was doing now, no matter how enjoyable Eamon made our encounters. It didn't feel right. It made me feel dirty and worst of all, it made me feel like a prostitute, which meant the pleasure he gave my body wore off fast as the guilt and disgust crept in. All of this could have been a quick and pleasurable encounter, *if* it had a chance in hell of helping my dad, which I knew now, it wouldn't.

I still wasn't sure how in the hell this arrangement helped Eamon, other than the fact he got four straight days of commitment free sex out of the deal. There was still the forty thousand dollars Dad owed, and no amount of earth-shattering sex would bring that money back. So really, what was the benefit of this for the infuriating man? He was gorgeous, powerful and rich so I was sure he had no shortage of women interested in warming his bed for a night or two. So what was his deal?

I had nowhere to go when I reached the mountains but drove toward them anyway, another fruitless gesture that would lead me nowhere but provided a small measure of comfort.

That comfort was short-lived though, as I noticed a sleek looking red car following me. Okay maybe not *following* me but the car had been behind me for miles, bypassing at least half a dozen exit ramps, rest stops, campsites, RV parks and other points of interest and it had stopped at none. Sure, neither had I but I was driving aimlessly and it was ... *not*.

Not that I thought I was so important that anyone would be following me, but right on the heels of that thought came another. What if the car had more guys my dad owed money to, thinking that a quick kidnapping might force him to pay up? Or worse, what if they wanted to kill me to show him they meant business? Neither of those scenarios worked out well for me, and I stepped on the gas.

At first, I felt silly when the car stayed far behind me, making no attempt to split the distance between us. Then the car sped up but it was so slowly that I might have thought I imagined it, if not for the fact that when I turned onto a ramp that lead to a rest stop, so did the sleek red car.

Without thinking twice, I hopped back to the on ramp and drove another few miles on the mostly deserted road, which suddenly seemed like a horrible idea, so I gunned it toward the next exit and swung around to make my way home.

I had another night of carnal bliss ahead of me, and though Eamon was by no means a good guy, at least I knew exactly what he wanted. Just my body for a few hours.

Nothing more.

And I was okay with that because he felt so damn good.

The red car appeared once more but the driver must have realized that the slow trickle of cars onto the freeway meant we were no longer alone. The downside was hella traffic on the way back to Rocket, but the upside was that I got to live for at least a few more hours.

This thing with my dad had apparently brought out my optimistic side. Or something.

Either way I was happy to head home even if I was less than happy about getting ready for another night with Eamon. Oh, I looked forward to the hours of bliss he provided, but tonight I just wanted to curl up in my pajamas, watch TV and drink some wine until I fell asleep on the sofa with the TV watching me. But that had to wait until next weekend.

Tonight, I still had a debt to pay.

Chapter Twenty

Eamon

Layla was late. She should've been here more than an hour ago yet here I sat on the sofa with a heavy crystal glass half full of whiskey in my hand. It was my third glass and so far, it hadn't done shit to calm my nerves or soothe my anger.

Not that I would blame Layla if she didn't show up. She'd found out a lot of shit about her father's problems and it surprised her. Terrified would be a more apt description, since I couldn't seem to forget the despair in her eyes or the way the tears she fought so hard to keep restrained hovered on the edge of her eyelids. She'd been devastated to find out that this wasn't the first time Peter had gotten himself into a deep hole he had no way in hell of getting out of. Surprisingly, I felt bad.

Not for Pete, but for his clueless daughter who didn't think twice about stepping in to help a man who didn't fucking deserve it. Not one fucking bit. I didn't deserve it either, but goddammit, I planned to reap all the benefits of having Layla in my bed, giving me the best, most enthusiastic sex of my fucking life.

I was no better than her father, the only difference was that her curves and her sweet, hot cunt was my vice. Not gambling or booze or drugs, though I dabbled in all of them on occasion. But women. *They* were my vice. When I'd had a bad day or an especially brutal one, I'd find a woman and fuck her for hours and hours until the bloody faces stopped appearing every fucking time I closed my eyes.

Some people might say I used those women, and I did, but there were no innocent victims in my bed. They all knew what they were getting into and what they could and couldn't expect. Even Layla, for all her legitimate complaints was no innocent. She went into this arrangement for a very specific reason. She wasn't being used here either. She was trying to be a fucking hero.

And she was ninety fucking minutes late.

We had a goddamn deal, four days and the debt was clear, and if I didn't get my days, the debt would stand and Peter Michaels wouldn't like what he'd have to do to pay it off. So I wasn't worried.

Anxious? Yeah.

Pissed off? Damn straight.

Worried? Fuck no.

My dick though, he was getting a little worried because just like me, he couldn't get enough of Layla and those sinful fucking curves that dared a man to give in to his most primal desires. When the security cameras showed the limo driving up the path I was on my feet, pacing the living room like a damned teenager.

"What the fuck am I doing?" My desire for this woman was worrisome. I couldn't remember the last time I wanted a woman the way I wanted Layla, my insatiable need for her driving me to do things I normally wouldn't.

The bell sounded and I stopped in my tracks and took two deep breaths before polishing off another glass of whiskey. Only when I had my shit under control did I pull open the door.

"Thought maybe you changed your mind."

It was a piss poor excuse for a greeting, I knew, but I had to know.

Layla shrugged and walked right by me in a pair of skintight jeans that showed off an ass she worked hard for, and thighs that were perfect for wrapping around my waist and sexy as fuck stilettos that I could only picture digging into my ass cheeks as I fucked her long and hard and deep.

"I needed to clear my head."

"Did you?"

"Mind making me a drink?" she asked instead of answering my question. "Whiskey neat is fine."

She eyed my glass and licked her lips, and just like that my feet were on the move and headed to the bar.

"Got a preference?" I looked over my shoulder and sucked in a breath at the sight that greeted me.

Fuck those skintight jeans that I ached to pull off because under that black leather jacket she wore a lacy pink top that cupped her tits magnificently. It was practically see-through, showing off a black bra, tons of cleavage, shoulders and chest. "Damn, girl."

"I prefer something strong. Make it a double."

"I don't fuck drunk chicks," I told her honestly.

"And you won't tonight, either."

The tension in the room was palpable. It was a living, breathing thing that sat in the room between us and made it impossible to even get a conversation started.

I poured two and a half fingers of whiskey into another glass, refilled mine and handed one to Layla. "Rough day?"

"Aren't they all?" She accepted her drink and took a long sip as she went to the wall of windows that showed nothing but the dense darkness of the wooded area behind my house. A weighted sigh blew out of her and Layla took another sip. And then another.

I couldn't put my finger on what it was exactly about Layla that got my heart rate accelerated and kept my dick hard all night long, but fuck it was addictive. I went to her, standing behind her without touching. Something was different about her tonight and I couldn't put my finger on it, but even her scent was different, lavender mixed with something, smelling of pure woman and sex.

"You always smell so good."

That sharp intake of breath hit my ears with delight and I smiled. "Thanks."

She jerked a little when one hand fell to her shoulder and slid up the side of her neck until it tangled in her hair.

"So soft," I moaned in her ear. I set my glass down to free my other hand, taking the same path from her silky bare shoulder to soft blonde waves. My fingers sifted through her hair, making Layla putty in my hands as she elicited little moans of pleasure. "Everywhere I touch you are so fucking soft." From her scalp I went to her shoulders, lightly massaging them until she could barely stand up on her own.

"Eamon," she moaned and tilted her head back, giving me perfect access to the gentle slope of her neck. Warm skin blended with sexy earth aromas that worked like a fucking aphrodisiac on me.

"Again," I growled. "Say it again." My teeth skid across the back of her neck and she shivered.

"Eamon. Please." Her plea was throaty and deep and the time for games was over. I spun her around and backed her up until she hit the cool glass window she was just looking out of. I slammed my mouth against hers. The kiss was a slow burn, heating up by degrees before it turned into a raging inferno of want and need, of lips and teeth and tongue, all fighting to get a better taste, a deeper kiss. More.

I gave her more of me and she took it, offering more of her mouth as I went deep and tasted every inch of her lips and tongue until she pulled back, panting with wide eyes that registered shock. And heat.

"Too much?"

A slow grin curved her lips. "Fuck no."

Thank fucking goodness for that. I slipped two fingers under the strap of her shirt and slid them both down until the black bra was revealed to me.

"Fuck me, Layla."

"On the agenda," she whispered with a little laugh.

She mumbled something else, but I didn't hear it because I was too fucking captivated by her lingerie. Black leather and lace with a ribbon tied behind her neck and nothing else to conceal her gorgeous cleavage. The lace fell over the swell of her breasts and when she turned, her whole back was on display, the contraption held together with a few more ribbons of fabric.

"Fuck this is hot."

She laughed again and looked up at me through thick, dark lashes, blue eyes sparkling with desire. "Glad you approve."

I more than approved but I was done talking. It was time to peel off those jeans and get a full look at the lingerie before I ripped it from her body and spent the rest of the night buried deep inside her. Tonight wasn't about taking it fast, at least not for me. My only plan was to keep Layla here all night. When she was in nothing but her sexy lingerie and those wickedly hot heels, which I put back on after I removed her jeans, I took a step back and watched.

"Sexy."

Layla's response was to lick her lips and cup her tits. "You think?"

"I know," I told her and closed the distance between us until she was once again pushed up against the window, shards of moonlight peeking through the only real light other than a few candles. Then I dipped low and found the stiff peak of her nipple and flicked my tongue against it through the fabric.

"Eamon," she moaned and arched her back into me.

I took everything she offered and then some because I was a greedy fucking bastard and I couldn't get enough of her. The more she cried and moaned and mewled her pleasure, the more I was so damn desperate to give to her. The taste of her through the sexy lingerie was intoxicating. I was tipsy from the whiskey, but I was drunk on Layla and I hadn't even tasted her sweet pussy yet.

"I need you. Just you."

The words were ripped out of me on a growl and I didn't give a damn how it sounded because all I gave a fuck about was getting my mouth on her. But first I had to strip the lace off her. Slowly.

With my teeth.

Finally she was naked but for those fucking heels that made her legs seem endless. On my knees in front of a woman was a place I rarely found myself, even when eating pussy but I was too fucking eager to get up close and personal with all of her.

"Eamon." She purred my name as her fingers tangled in my hair. And tightened. Her gaze so intense I didn't know whether to thrust into her or reach for my gun, she licked her lips so slowly my cock began to leak.

"Please."

I smiled and grabbed her ankle, never taking my eyes off her as I placed open mouth kisses from her ankle up to the center of her thighs. Then I did it to the other leg.

"So soft." I inhaled the new scent of her, lavender and arousal, and something flowery that was all Layla.

"You wet for me Layla?"

I knew she would be, the air was thick with her scent but I wanted to hear her say it.

"I don't know, am I?" She hissed out a breath when slid my thumb between slick, swollen lips. "Ah!" She quivered.

"Soaked."

She wanted this as much as I did and nothing was hotter than a woman who knew what she wanted, especially in bed, and wasn't afraid to ask for it.

"Hold yourself open for me."

She held my gaze, a smile shining in her eyes as her hands slid down her body until they reached between her legs and exposed her hard clit to me. "Bon Appetit!"

I chuckled and she smiled along with me until my tongue flicked out and sent her head falling back against the window with a thud. My mouth took over and Layla kept my cock hard with a steady stream of moans and cries, "oh fucks," and my personal favorite, "fuck yeah." I lifted one curvy leg over my shoulder and her gaze found me again, dark and hungry.

"Don't come," I warned her when I felt her legs start to tremble.

She let out a strangled groan. "Are you crazy? I'm about ten licks ... nine licks away. Eight," she moaned, panted and reached a hand to grip my hair. "Eamon, oh!"

"Don't. Come."

I knew she wouldn't listen when her hand tightened around my hair hard enough to sting but when she began to grind her pussy back and forth against my lips and my tongue, I didn't give a shit. Watching her from below as she took her pleasure, eyes glued to mine as she fucked my face, watching her come apart nearly had me coming in my jeans.

Nearly.

But there was no fucking way after Layla fucked my face that I would come anywhere but in her tight, wet cunt.

"You're so good at that," she whimpered.

I laughed, still licking her as I unwrapped her leg and set her foot on the floor. "Thanks. Come here."

I wasn't in the mood to talk, not with my cock so hard all I could hear was blood pumping in my ears.

"I'm here," she purred and wrapped an arm around me. "Now what?"

I gripped her hips and lifted her in the air and spun in a circle two or three times in search of a flat surface for what I had in mind. I fucking hated the decorative tables planted all around the room full of little tchotchkes, but right now I might give my decorator a raise. Layla hissed out a breath when her back hit the cool surface of the table, arching into me. I pulled a nipple in my mouth and sucked. Hard.

"Fuck!" Her nipples were bright red, slick and swollen and I only wanted to go back for more.

"Eamon," she moaned and tightened her legs around my waist, grinding her pussy against my denim covered cock. "Fuck me."

I nibbled my way down her body, scraping my teeth across her nipples, ribs, hipbones until I was far enough away to get undressed. Layla sat up on her elbows and watched liked it was a goddamn striptease.

"Enjoying the show?"

"You know what you look like without clothes."

"But I don't know what you think about how I look without clothes." I smiled at her and she spread her legs barely an inch, just enough for the moonlight to catch a sliver of moisture on her lips.

She sighed. "I think you look damn good naked. The rare man who looks better without clothes."

My cock sprang free at her words, straining and jerking toward her and she laughed.

"Happy?"

"Fucking ecstatic," I told her and gripped my cock, running the head up and down her pussy, letting her juices coat my cock. "So, so wet."

"That's on ... you."

She said the last word on a moan as I slid slowly into her, pausing after every inch to look at her simply because I couldn't take my eyes off her.

"More," she begged.

One jerk of my hips and my cock was buried deep with no air between us. Layla cried out and her pussy clamped around me.

"Shit," I hissed. I couldn't stop touching her, even as I touched her in the most intimate way possible. My hands skated up her legs and over the curve of her ass, the dip of her waist and up to those fantastic tits. Every inch of flesh my hands touched turned my dick to steel until it was agonizing.

"Fuck. Layla, fuck."

"More, Eamon. Fuck me. Harder."

I let out a low groan and pounded harder into her, letting my hand slide up to her throat for a small squeeze. I watched as her hooded eyes flared wide for a split second but more importantly, I felt the way her pussy crushed my cock, pulsing quickly all around me. "Oh fuck!" I cried.

Layla grabbed at my wrist and I prepared myself for her to shove it away but she didn't. Her grip tightened on my wrist and my grip tightened just a hair. She pulsed around me again and I snapped.

My hips took over, pumping in and out of her, one hand fondling her breast while the other held her throat. I couldn't look away because every emotion, every expression of pleasure was written all over her face and telegraphed to my cock. Tighter and tighter she gripped me and I knew she was close.

"Yes," she squeaked out unnecessarily.

Her legs tightened as her pleasure took over and I continued to pump into her, hard and fast, until pleasure snaked up my spine and my orgasm was yanked from the depths of my nutsac. It was rough and vicious, and long, pulling every ounce of pleasure from me it could.

"Fuck yeah, baby."

Chapter Twenty-One

Layla

There were two things I noticed when I woke up from a knock-out orgasm. First, I was still totally bare assed naked, and second, there was a big, strong, manly arm banded around my waist. Neither of which were common occurrences in my life worth mentioning. It took half a second to remember that the arm belonged to Eamon, not because we just couldn't keep our hands off each other, even if that was true, but that I was here to pay a debt.

I blinked and looked out the window to see the night dotted with sparkling stars and the moon lighting up the room just enough to see the outline of Eamon's shoulder. Even in sleep he was a powerful man. His muscles shone under the moonlight, giving his skin a pale yellow hue. I turned, careful not to wake him because I wanted to see if he was as intimidating in his sleep as he was awake.

Yep. Eyes closed, bed head, and the slow, rhythmic breathing did nothing to weaken him. I was sure if his eyes were open, they'd be as fierce and implacable as they always were.

But now with them closed, I could have my fill of him. Take in all the details I'd missed, including that small scar on his left eyebrow and the scar on his abdomen that could have been a stab wound or a bullet wound. Either was plausible and as I let my hand roam over that scar, I closed my mind to the gruesome thoughts and images of how he got it.

"Christ, that's a lot of thinking when the sun's not even up yet." Eamon turned his head and opened his eyes with one eyebrow arched in question.

"Even if it's thinking about giving you a wake-up blow job?" I hadn't been thinking about it but now that I'd said it, my body was already gearing up for the show.

"Never too early for those kinds of thoughts. Or too late. Were you?"

I shook my head with a teasing smile. "No. I was really thinking about when you let me ride your face earlier. God, I even had a dream about it. I think I might have picked up a new fetish."

Eamon tighten his hold on me, hands digging into my ass as he fit me against him with a tortured groan. "You can ride my face anytime you like, princess."

I felt the blush creep up my chest and by the time it turned my scalp pink, the heat flamed hotter. "I just might take you up on that."

He grinned and closed his eyes, pulling me half way on top of him while his fingertips played up and down the dip in the center of my back. It was a soft touch, a lover's touch that felt too good considering what we were. What *this* was. "Hungry?"

"Starved." I'd eaten five bites of the delicious pastrami before the whole printer debacle took up most of my afternoon and that was the sum total of my food consumption for the day.

"Come on. There's always something in the fridge."

"That's a nice perk. We sure do eat a lot," I said, accepting the oversized t-shirt he threw at me and following him into the kitchen. "Do fairies come in and pick your towels up off the floor, too?"

He grinned up at me. It was cute and boyish and I really wished I hadn't seen it. "Gotta stay strong. And who says I leave my towels on the floor?"

"You don't?" I challenged him, my gaze on the beautiful expanse of his back. His muscles were beautifully sculpted and his arms were the perfect canvas.

"I do, but I pay Loretta very well to come in and be my fairy three times a week."

"Sounds kinky."

Eamon barked out a laugh and let my nails dig deep into my palms because when he was relaxed, free of his gangster persona, he was irresistible. "I'll tell Loretta you said so and her husband of thirty years."

"Wow. That's a long time to be married."

"You sound envious." His tone was curious but there was a hint of caution in them.

"I am. I envy the kind of trust it takes to be with someone so fully. Sometimes I wonder what kind of lives those people have."

But I never wondered too hard because finding out they somehow had it harder than me would mean *I* was the problem.

"Didn't peg you as a romantic." He said it like it was a dirty word and I couldn't help but smile as he pulled out ingredients for sandwiches from the fridge.

"Not a romantic, just a realist. It would be nice to have that but I don't think I could ever trust anyone enough."

And thank you Dad for adding another layer on top of my trust issues.

"You might find this hard to believe Eamon, but when I turn fifty, I won't have a gaggle of twenty-something guys lining up to bang me."

His heated gaze turned to confusion and then he scoffed. "You think I'm fifty?"

That hint of vulnerability was damned appealing. What was so fucking wrong with me that every broken piece of himself he revealed only made me want him more?

"I think it doesn't matter how old you are. You're good looking and you have that whole bad boy thing going with the added bonus of being an actual bad boy, plus rich. You have the luxury of being an eternal bachelor."

"Mustard?"

"Spicy?"

He nodded and I nodded back, enjoying how utterly sexy and masculine he looked wearing nothing but a pair of low slung pajama pants while he made big fancy deli sandwiches.

"You said you would never trust anyone, Layla."

"That doesn't mean I'm not open to the possibility of it. So far it hasn't happened and I have little hope that'll change anytime soon."

As it stood, if a man was attracted to me that was a guarantee that he was no good. Homeless, unemployed, married, a musician, permanent students and gay rounded out the problems with my exes over the years.

"You have great sandwich skills, by the way."

He grinned and sliced the sandwich diagonally, dropping a pickle on each plate along with a handful of chips. "Easy and perfect any time of day."

"But you have a chef."

"I do, but I keep odd hours sometimes and other times I just want to be on my own. Do my own thing."

His words were sincere. A rich guy who didn't enjoy having a herd of servants around to dote on him. "So Eamon, do you have siblings and cousins who are also your best friends?"

He grinned like a caught little kid. "How'd you know?"

"I didn't but I'm trying to see how much gangster stuff is real and how much is fiction."

He looked up, sandwich halfway to his mouth and grinned. "Seriously?"

"Why not? This stuff is legendary and when am I ever going to get a chance to ask these questions again?"

He gave me that look, that sort of condescending yet affectionate one you get from an older brother's best friend. Not that I was familiar with it personally, but I kept my e-reader stocked with romance books, so I kind of had a good idea.

After a long pause he finally answered. "Yes. I have a younger brother and a cousin. I don't know if we're best friends, but we are very close."

"That sounds nice. Mom and Dad were both only children with elderly parents so holidays were small. Quiet."

He pointed to himself before he swallowed, then answered. "Boisterous, bordering on obnoxious would describe our family gatherings." He grinned again, this one loving as he described his family. "It can get loud and crazy but it's the way things have always been."

"You like it," I accused, and he shrugged.

"I do. My family means everything to me."

"Clearly." I said, a little snarkier than intended.

His face hardened as anger changed his features back to the slab of stone they usually were. "I won't apologize for doing my job, Layla."

"I'm not asking you to." In fact, I hadn't asked anything other than some stupid mob questions, even though the more I was around him the more I wanted to know about him and his real life. "Thanks for the sandwich."

I slid off the stool and tugged down his t-shirt. "I'm gonna get out of here."

No point ruining another amazing orgasm with an argument. Eamon sat in silence, and I blamed my love of romance novels for making me wish he'd said something while I rinsed off my plate and glass. I didn't even look at him when I left the kitchen.

Eamon was an island. He didn't need anyone not born with the last name Connelly. More importantly, he didn't want them.

"Stay."

Damn him! That one word had the power to undo me completely.

I should have listened carefully to the warning bells that sounded in my head. The really loud ones. I really should have fucking listened.

***

"This is no morning blowjob but I ain't complaining."

I didn't know what came over me but after that delicious sandwich and two more soul-crushing orgasms, in the kitchen and then on the stairs, we fell into a dreamless heap on the bed. But when I woke up hours later with the sun cutting through the large windows of Eamon's bedroom, I felt a desperate need to have him.

The need came and it was urgent, like something had possessed me to just take what I wanted. I turned and saw Eamon and in that one split second, he was all I wanted and, still naked from the night before, my hand started a slow, rhythmic caress on his already hardening cock.

I wanted him with a hunger I couldn't explain. Maybe it was because this was our last few moments together before we went off and lived the rest of our lives completely ignorant of what the other would be doing. Or maybe it was that my body was addicted to the painful pleasure found in his bed. I couldn't explain it, and honestly, I had no desire to explain or examine it. All I wanted was to experience it. Enjoy it.

And I was.

I swung my leg over him and guided his cock to my entrance. Looking down at him, his eyes sleepy and his mouth curved into a lazy grin, I couldn't tear my eyes away. He was beautiful in a way that a man shouldn't be, not when he was a sex-trading mobster I caught beating the shit out of my dad.

"Layla."

His head rolled back as his hands tightened on my hips, and he thrusted deeper into me until he was so deep, such a part of me, that real worry settled low in my belly. Was I developing feelings for this man?

"No!"

Eamon's eyes flew open and he froze mid-stroke and another, embarrassing kind of fear gripped me.

"You okay?"

I nodded quickly and tightened around him. "Just ... it feels too good."

"Nothing feels *too* good, princess." He punctuated the words by drawing back and stroking deep inside me, touching parts of me I didn't know existed.

Another loud groan tore from his throat and Eamon grinned.

"Okay you do feel damn good."

I felt the smile the moment it touched my lips and forced my hips to move. I tossed my head back, unwilling to let him see just how much his words pleased me.

"Right back at you."

I didn't want to talk, not when he filled me so deliciously. Not when our bodies communicated every single thing we needed to say to each other.

We didn't need words, not when his eyes spoke of endless pleasure and his grip told the tale of possessiveness. It was different. *I* was different that morning. Bold and daring, confident, even as his fucking shook me to my core, sending pesky emotions best left alone skittering to the surface. It was slow and sensual, the kind of sex that people wrote songs about, with lots of guitar and maybe even a saxophone.

"You still with me, Layla?"

I nodded and ground my hips faster and faster, chasing down the pleasure that wouldn't be stopped until it made me its bitch, a fiend who wouldn't stop until I had experienced total fucking bliss.

"Right ... there!"

His thumb went to my clit, an unnecessary but not unwelcome addition to the wave of pleasure determined to carry me away. Back and forth, around and around my hips went, a rhythm of their own creation. I moved faster, grinding on him until sweat dripped down my spine, until his hands could barely grip my breasts, they were so slick from our coming together that we were just sliding against each other like animals as we both barreled toward sweet, satisfying pleasure.

Only there was nothing sweet or satisfying about the pleasure that dropped on me like ten tons of water. It was hard and visceral, instinctual as our bodies continued to bump and grind and claw at each other, frantic for those last threads of pleasure. His body jerked with his orgasm and mine tensed, sending him deeper and triggering a second wave of pleasure before the first was complete.

Eamon chuckled as I collapsed on top of him, his hands circled my waist and then he surprised the hell out of me when his fingertips began to dance over my heated flesh.

"That was unexpected."

I didn't respond. I couldn't, mostly because I was still trying to suck down some oxygen but also because emotion clogged my throat. And I wasn't having any of that.

Damn, the sex was too good. I knew the trouble with good dick and great sex. They made women stupid. Perfectly reasonable women were made irrational and emotional when it came to a man who could make their clit swell and toes curl on command. I refused to let myself be that woman, so I slapped a smile on face and sat up so I could look down at Eamon.

"Not that unexpected, it's what I'm here for, right?"

He looked confused and the minute I tried to get away by leaping from the bed, he held me down, our bodies still connected.

"What's that supposed to mean?"

"Nothing. It was great. Hot and amazing. Incredible as always but it wasn't really unexpected. Was it?"

He sighed, apparently annoyed that I'd mucked up his post-orgasmic glow with a bit of realism. "Fine, it wasn't. Happy? Or do you want a big fight to make you feel better about enjoying yourself?"

I tried to wiggle my way free of Eamon's grip, which seemed a pretty fitting metaphor for what was going through me as my gaze slammed into his ice-cold stare.

"Damn, Eamon. I'm not trying to start a fight and the sex was great, so there's no need for an ulterior motive. Just stating a fucking fact."

He released me and I scrambled off the bed like it was on fire. It might as well have been as far as I was concerned. Eamon's hand had felt like a brand and everywhere he'd touched felt cool and lonely without his warmth. No, dammit! I shook it off and looked at him, doing my best not to feel vulnerable or humiliated standing there butt naked.

"Bullshit."

His cool dismissal made it easy to remember that we were nothing but a fuck to each other. And yeah, that thought might have stung a little but I knew from experience that the aftermath of a guy like him hurt far worse.

"Doesn't matter anyway. We're done here."

I gave his big, ultra masculine bedroom a final sweep to make sure I didn't forget anything I couldn't live without because there was no way in hell I'd ever come back here.

"For today, yes."

I'd already taken a few steps outside the bedroom because my clothes were still by the bank of windows in the main room when his words registered. They stopped me in my tracks.

"No, for good. Today is Saturday. Day four."

I didn't think it took a lot of brains to become a mobster, especially when it was your family's mob or whatever, but this was ridiculous.

"Day. Four." Was he trying not to laugh at me? "Something funny?"

"You have a shit poker face just like your old man."

"That's fine because I don't play poker."

"Yeah, yeah," he said dismissively and swung his legs around the side of the bed, his cock was still flying at half staff. And still leaking. Damn. "It's a good thing too since your thoughts are written all over your face."

"Again, irrelevant. Goodbye, Eamon." I turned on my heels with my stilettos in hand and padded down the hall on my bare feet so I could get my clothes and get the hell out of here. For good.

"Goodbye for now." His smooth voice, deep and seductive, sounded behind me making my core tighten and my nipples bead with arousal.

"Today might be the fourth day, princess, but it marks the end of the third night."

I turned to him, ready to argue my case when he held up a hand that pulled me up short. "Wednesday, Thursday and then last night. Three days."

"What about the limo ride at my office? Doesn't that count for anything?"

"It counts for a good fuck. But the agreement was four nights. Not three nights and a quickie."

"A quickie?" I snorted. "Okay, you know what? You win." I was actually more excited than pissed off to find out we had one more night together. That was as sure a sign as any that I needed to get away from him and fast. I located my lingerie and slid it on and then my jeans and shirt, scooping my stilettos as I darted past him. "I'll see you tonight, Eamon."

"Unless you don't want to?"

I barked out a laugh. "As if it matters what I want at this point. I'll see you tonight."

"I'll take you home." His tone brooked no argument and even if I'd planned to argue, which I did, he was halfway down the hall, presumably to put some clothes on.

"I can get home myself, you know!" Two seconds later the shower came on, just in case I didn't already know he wasn't listening. It was a meaningless gesture, but I grabbed my purse and fled out the front door, coming up short because there was no limo waiting.

Dammit.

Chapter Twenty-Two

Eamon

"Is this car necessary?" Layla's green eyes bore a hole in the side of my head even as her hands couldn't stop molesting the buttery soft leather seat. "I mean, what is the purpose of this car?"

Her words tugged a reluctant laugh from me. As a rule I didn't explain myself to anyone but Patrick and especially not to women. Then again, I couldn't remember a time when a woman had ever criticized one of my vehicles. "Purpose? To go fast and look good doing it. Isn't that enough?"

A husky laugh sprang free and she smacked a hand against my thigh, making my leg twitch. "If that's your goal, mission accomplished but you have to admit that it *is* kind of ridiculous."

"You're calling my Bugatti Vision GT ridiculous? I think you'd better take a look in the mirror sweetheart." This car was a goddamn work of art. Royal blue and black with shiny chrome wheels.

"I'm sure it's a real boner inducer for a certain kind of guy but it's got four wheels and an engine. Does it really need all this?"

She waved her arms around the interior and laughed again.

"Okay sure, it's pretty. But also ridiculous."

"I'm a car guy. I collect them. You prefer the limo?"

"At least the limo is appropriately ridiculous." Her hands scrubbed over the leather again with a smile. "I do love this leather though. I'd kill to turn this into a skirt."

She would look damned hot in this blue leather with her long legs on display. "So not so ridiculous after all?"

"Still ridiculous, but I'm starting to get the appeal. A little." Her hands slid up and down the leather a few more times. "So you like cars?"

"I like all machines. Cars, motorcycles, boats ..."

"Yachts, you mean?"

I shrugged. "Boats of all sizes."

She laughed again and the sound bounced around the inside of the car, adding an unexpected warmth.

"Yachts. Do you know how to drive a boat or whatever?"

"I know my way around quite a few different boats. Speed boats, yachts, sail boats. I don't like to be inside something I can't navigate if I need to."

"Of course," she snorted and rolled her eyes. "God forbid."

The car stopped in the spot beside Layla's car and she darted out of the car before I even killed the engine.

"Layla, wait!" She kept going, eager to escape for some reason.

"Dammit, Layla."

I cut the engine and caught up to her at the top of the stairs and reached for her arm. "What the hell?"

She smiled but it didn't come close to reaching her big blue eyes. "Thank you for the ride, Eamon. I'll see you tonight."

Oh fuck that. "Not good enough, princess."

Her expression changed as she jerked away from my grasp. "Then it's a good thing I don't owe you a damn explanation, isn't it?"

Ah, kitten wanted to play? I backed her up against the wall, not giving a damn whose door I had her pressed up against, my leg between her thighs.

"You don't owe me an explanation, but I want one anyway."

"Too. Bad." That's what her mouth said but one little tug of her earlobes between my teeth and she was moaning, melting into me.

"Tell me."

"Tell you what?"

She was already breathless and panting, that little pulse in her neck beating a drum solo.

"Why you're running away from me."

Layla pulled back and licked her lips.

"I'm not running away, Eamon. Just going home." She slid between me and the wall, walking a few short feet to her door, but I grabbed her arm at the last minute and pulled her back to me.

"Looks like running to me." I cut off her denial with a kiss, holding her at the waist with one hand as I tangled my fingers in her hair with the other, my mouth devouring hers. It was dark and hot and something else I couldn't describe but it didn't matter because her taste got better every fucking time.

"See you tonight, princess. Seven p.m."

She looked too dazed to keep her walls up and her eyes were filled with something I hadn't seen in a long time. Affection.

"Don't call me that," she said but her words lacked their usual fire and I knew she was getting ideas.

"Better get those stars out of your eyes, Layla."

The sparkle in her eyes dimmed and she took another step away from me. "Those aren't stars, dork, that's just a post-orgasm glow."

She put a fake smile on her face and batted her eyelashes. Then, without a look back, Layla walked away and slammed her door shut.

Engaging *both* locks.

Message fucking received.

She was pissed off now, but by the time night fell she would be aching for me to fill her, the same way I ached for her already.

One more night and Layla would be nothing more than a smoking hot memory. Then my life would be back to normal.

As I got back in my car and drove home, all I could think about was how suddenly normal didn't seem all that appealing.

Chapter Twenty-Three

Layla

I felt out of sorts after Eamon kissed the hell out of me, so I took a quick hot shower until his scent no longer lingered on my skin and my body only burned from the scalding water and not his touch.

The whole Saturday stretched ahead of me. I got dressed and sat around my house in search of something to do or someone to talk to. I'd been too busy building my career and taking care of Dad that I didn't have any real close friends, just a few acquaintances I could go out drinking with when I needed to unwind. My apartment was in order, so I couldn't do a few hours of mindless cleaning to keep me busy, either.

I went to the gym and spent thirty minutes on the treadmill pounding out anything that might resemble feelings or emotions. I ran out the anger I felt at my dad for keeping this huge thing from me and then for letting it get so bad that it got to this point. I ran out the feelings that were bubbling just beneath the surface for Eamon. I ran and ran, then I swam, focusing on nothing but the next stroke through the water. But even ninety minutes at the gym couldn't tire out my overeager mind.

Which meant I needed to venture outside again, something I had no desire to do while I still felt raw and a little shaken by my time with Eamon. But maybe a bit of grocery shopping with a few hours of retail therapy was exactly what I needed, at least that was my excuse when I grabbed my purse and reusable bags and got in my car.

Rocket wasn't a big metropolis by any stretch of the imagination but a girl had options. There were two malls in addition to all the shops and boutiques inside the two dozen or so casinos in town. I turned out of the parking lot and got ready to blast Queen Bey when I saw something that stopped me cold. At first I didn't even realize what it was, but my body recognized it before I did.

The sleek red car that I saw yesterday rolled down my street at a much slower speed than most drivers use. It didn't matter much that there was no reason for anyone to be following me but tell that to my overactive imagination that had me convinced they were sex traffickers looking for pretty young girls to sell to rich dudes overseas.

Since there was clearly no way to reason with me, had anyone been with me to reason with, I reversed out of my parking spot and sped away like a bat out of hell. I drove and drove, my eyes flying to my side mirrors and my rearview mirror like I was the getaway driver for a bank heist. If there were any cops around, I would've been pulled over and given at least three tickets, but the traffic goddesses were smiling down on me because there wasn't a black and white in sight.

I merged into the traffic at the mega shopping center complete with the biggest supermarket in town, which was surrounded by at least two dozen stores, shops and boutiques.

My heart still raced, even as I threw the car in park and rested my head on the steering wheel.

"No one is following me. I'm being ridiculous."

My emotions had to have been on edge if I thought some random red car was the same car as yesterday *and* following me through Rocket, Nevada. "Yeah, right."

A laugh bubbled out of me at just how silly I was being and how real my fear was. The laughter helped and with one final look around, I stepped from the car with my handy canvas bags and got lost in rampant consumerism for a few hours.

Mostly rampant consumerism mixed in with a sickening dose of obsessing over a certain hard bodied gangster. Why couldn't I stop thinking about him? He wasn't my boyfriend or some guy I met in a bar and hooked up with a few times or any variation of that scenario. Nope, he was a guy who'd demanded my body in payment for a debt.

No more and no less.

But still, when I thought of last night, which I did for damn near the entire afternoon, I swore there were flashes of emotion there. Something beyond lust and desire, more than simple pleasure seeking. But it could have been the pleasure he gave me that was clouding my vision and making me see things that weren't there. It wouldn't be the first time I'd made that particular mistake and I swore after the second time, I was done with that. But that was said with the bravado of a twenty-two-year-old and in the three years since I made that teary promise, I hadn't broken it.

Not. Even. Once.

And I wouldn't this time either. Just because my stupid heart was seeing things and making me feel things that I absolutely did not want to, didn't mean I had to say anything or act on it. I didn't. I wouldn't. In fact, I doubled back to the baking goods aisle to pick up some chocolate chips, flour and nuts so I would have something sweet waiting for me when I came home from Eamon's. Tonight.

My last night with him.

I repeated that speech to myself while I packed the groceries into my trunk and again when I brought the bags in to the kitchen and baked my sweet treats. It became my mantra for the rest of the afternoon. And it worked.

Mostly.

When I forgot to remind myself, my mind inevitably wandered back to him, but I was good, and I quickly shut that shit down.

It wasn't much but it was a start.

A damn good start.

Chapter Twenty-Four

Eamon

Forty thousand dollars wasn't a lot of money. Sure, to the average working stiff it was a full year of taking shit from some middle manager, two weeks of vacation time and endless meetings that made him want to kill himself, but it still wasn't a lot of money.

I knew to Layla it was a lot of money, and I knew how it made her feel to fuck me to clear that debt, but it was an unimpressive amount. And when you saw it all together it was just four stacks, each containing one hundred pieces of paper with Benjamin Franklin's face smiling at you.

On top of the stack was another five hundred bucks. Exactly the amount Peter Michaels owed.

"Is there anything else I can do for you Mr. Connelly?" The pretty bank manager gave me a professional smile, keeping her distance like a smart woman.

"No thank you Natalie. I'm set." Her gaze slid to the now closed safe deposit box and back to my face.

"Very good, Mr. Connelly." We locked the box and she escorted me to the door with a smile and a friendly, "See you again real soon." It was folksy as hell but a nice touch.

So said Patrick when she gave him the same routine.

Cash in hand, I made my way to the car and ripped off the bands, balling up a few bills, rolling some between rubber bands and shoving it all into a convenience store paper bag. My dad would be pleased and that was all that mattered.

Patrick was waiting in the over the top sun room when I arrived. "I thought you might have had more important things to do than meet with your ol' da." Sometimes, for no discernible reason, Patrick would speak in a stilted Irish accent.

"It's still Saturday, isn't it?" I flashed a grin and though his wrinkled eyes were still keen as hell, his smile was the one I'd known all my life.

"It is. You look well rested."

"So do you for once." The old man refused to slow down even though his body wasn't quite as sharp as his mind was, which was to say his big frame no longer held the fifty extra pounds of muscle it had in his younger days.

"Yeah, that Ambien is better than whiskey and a cigar. Who knew?" Another ghost of a grin flashed before his expression turned to business.

"Got something for me?"

"I do." I nodded and handed him the paper bag, standing there in front of his desk like a child waiting to be scolded as he counted it out. By hand. Twice.

"Good job son. I can always count on you to get the job done."

"Yeah, you can."

He gave a sharp nod, the only sign he would ever give that he was impressed. "Shae and Rourke are waiting in the dining room, we'd better hurry before they eat all our lunch."

"Lunch?" Though we usually ate family dinner on Sundays unless work kept us busy, it was rare for all four of us to sit down to a meal any other time. "What's up?"

Patrick stood to his full height, so we were almost eye-to-eye. "You'll find out soon enough."

And I knew that was that. Patrick didn't reveal any information any sooner than he deemed it necessary. It was a damn frustrating part of working with my father that no one ever told me, his weird little eccentricities that weren't a huge problem at the breakfast table could make life irritating as hell as an adult. "Fine. Keep your secrets."

"We all have secrets, son. Just make sure they're not the kind that get you a desert grave." And with that he entered the kitchen with me behind him wondering what kind of trouble was about to fall on our heads because nothing but family matters would get Patrick riled up.

And he was riled up. It was the stiff set of his broad, square shoulders, those tiny lines of tension around his mouth as he took the head of the table and I took the spot to his right. "I taught you boys well if you didn't devour everything in sight."

"I had breakfast at Ma's," Rourke said by way of explanation for his empty plate.

"I had some leftovers in the kitchen." Shae smiled, looking relaxed as always in his seat beside me.

"Well fill up your plates, we have business to discuss." Business could mean anything from some guy harassing Aunt Fiona to one of our businesses being audited by the tax man.

The dining room fell silent as it always did for the first few minutes of any family meal while Patrick gave thanks and then we all grabbed a little bit of everything from potatoes to bacon and cabbage, roast chicken, bread, spiced beef and my favorite, colcannon.

"Such a huge feast on a Saturday, what's up, Uncle?" Rourke asked before he took a bite of bread.

"Bad news," Patrick began and stopped with a dramatic pause while he took a sip of whiskey. "The Milano brothers have been seen around Rocket."

"Which brothers?"

"Does it matter?" Patrick's eyebrows arched in question, baiting me to tell him what I thought.

"You know it does. Gio and Frank are kids, doing stupid shit that draws too much fucking heat." It mattered because the younger Milano twins, Lorenzo's grandsons, were barely twenty and they were crazy as fuck. Reckless.

"And ...?" Patrick taunted, always testing and teasing.

"And Daniel knows how to handle his business. Angelo is all right. A little crazy, but he cleans up good. If Lorenzo sent the twins, then he's just swinging his little dick, but if he sent his older sons, he's making a real play."

It was simple fucking business and I'd do the exact same thing if I had to.

"Maybe they came to steal some of our ideas for their new gaming lounge?" Shae offered, protective of the project he'd been handed with a neat little bow tied around it.

"What if I told you it was Gio and Angelo?" Patrick's silence to my question spoke more than his words could have. Or should have.

"Damn. That motherfucking Lorenzo is trying to train the fuck out of Angelo," Rourke offered between bites.

"Probably both of them. And considering how reckless they are, he probably hopes one of them straightens up before they both wind up dead. I'm surprised we haven't seen Daniel. That motherfucker is the one he should be training. He's smarter and more level headed than Angelo."

I was also surprised they hadn't landed themselves in the morgue yet. Then again, maybe they were waiting on me to put them there.

"I want eyes on them until they get the fuck out of Rocket."

Patrick's expression was serious, and I pulled my phone out, connecting with a couple of my guys who handled security for the family.

"Rascal and his men will let me know as soon as they have eyes on the Milano brothers."

Rascal was the best finder around. If someone was lost, taken, or voluntarily fell off the grid, Rascal and his men could find them. WitSec, CIA, and the Feds all around the world feared him, which was exactly why we kept him on the payroll.

"Good." He nodded and dug into his plate with the energy of a man half his age. "I want to know every fucking thing they do in town, where they're staying and exactly when they leave my city."

"You got it." My phone was never turned off, which meant as soon as Rascal's call came in, I'd know it. "Consider it taken care of."

"I have," he said simply and returned to his meal just like the rest of us, soaking up the peace and quiet that could only be found when a group of men got together for a delicious meal.

"That was good, Uncle Patrick. I hate to eat and run but I promised Ma I'd help her around the house today."

Patrick smiled. "You're a good man, Rourke. Always looking after your ma the way you do. Tell Fiona I look forward to her lamb tomorrow."

"It's already marinating in the fridge."

"You should all have a sister like mine," he proclaimed with a satisfied smile. Patrick finished his food and stood. "I have a visitor coming in exactly one hour, so I expect you all gone in the next thirty minutes."

The thought of what the old man was up to was enough to get us all on our feet and heading toward the door in under a minute.

That was just fine by me since I needed to get things ready for my last night with Layla.

Chapter Twenty-Five

Layla

There was something freeing about spending a few hours in the kitchen, baking my favorite batches of cookie bars so they'd be nice and soft by the time I came back home. A bunch of veggies were all set up in the slow cooker, ready to begin a lengthy cooking process that I would have very little to do with, which meant they would come out edible. And I'd have dinner for tomorrow along with lunch for a few days next week. It was nice, really. Helped clear my mind and steel myself for a night of nothing but sex. Nothing but a physical release.

No emotions and no goddamn stars in my eyes.

Okay maybe there were still a few lingering stars that sat on my shoulders and whispered in my ear, *"Tell him how you feel."* Or crazy things like, *"What's the worst that could happen?"*

I ignored the voices or at least I tried to. It was just that the idea of seeing Eamon again excited me.

This was a clear-cut case of my stupid heart trying to take the reins when I'd already decided that my brain should run the show. And that was exactly what I convinced myself of when I stepped under the hot shower spray to get ready for tonight. It was crazy to even consider broaching the subject with Eamon. He'd made it beyond clear earlier with his *stars in your eyes* comment exactly how he felt about me developing a case of *inconvenient* feelings for him.

His voice had been a low, cool warning. *I'm not what you want, trust me.* Except he was. For some reason I wanted the fucker, or rather my heart wanted him no matter how fucked up and mean I tried to make him sound.

I picked out my clothes for the evening carefully, making sure I looked good but not like I was trying to look good for him. I wasn't.

Okay, maybe I was.

A pair of black jeans with a sheer black top would keep it simple yet sexy. Underneath I'd wear a lingerie set that would make him sorry to see me go.

My mind swirled with at least thirty different ways he might reject me, starting with laughter and ending with blind rage. The truth was I knew nothing about Eamon and most of what I knew came from the news and the few bits of information he'd actually shared with me over the past few days.

"No one has ever died from a broken heart."

My mom used to say that to me whenever I'd cry over not getting my way and I smiled at the memory.

It was like she showed up to drop a dollop of wisdom on me just when I needed it the most. Mom was right, no one ever died from a broken heart, at least no one I knew. If, in some alternate universe, I told Eamon that I had feelings for him and he rejected me, it'd probably hurt like hell. But my heart wouldn't stop beating and the world wouldn't stop turning on its axis. I might cry a little and drown my sorrows in booze and junk food for a few days, but then, I'd get over it.

I'd move on with my life.

Easy peasy.

I grabbed my black shoes with the thick black ribbons around the ankles. They were guaranteed to drive Eamon wild and that was exactly the version of him I wanted for our last night together. So yeah, I would tell him.

The bell rang as I made my way down the hall and I smiled, thinking maybe I wasn't the only one eager for tonight after all. The closer I got to the door, the more sure I was that spilling my emotional guts to Eamon was exactly what I would do. No matter what happened, I would do it.

I would survive it.

No matter what.

I pulled the door open with a smile that quickly died when I came face to face with a very large man with carrot red hair I didn't recognize smoking a cigar.

"Can I help you?"

"Hi, Layla."

He blew a puff of smoke in my face and I took a step back, gripping the doorknob in my fist.

"Don't blow smoke in my face, asshole!"

He sighed and sucked in another breath. "It's your lucky day little lady."

Something about the guy didn't seem right and it wasn't just that he looked rough, with about four days worth of stubble on his cheeks or the slightly sweat stained t-shirt he wore. It was the twitchy way he had about him, the uneasiness that sat on his shoulders.

"I don't have time for your games," I barked at him. With a roll of my eyes I slammed the door in his face.

Correction, I *tried* to slam the door in his face, but his big meaty hand reached out and grabbed it, pushing it back hard enough that the edge smacked me right in the face.

"Son of a bitch!" I shrieked, a shock of pain streaking across my nose as I fell to the floor.

"Shoulda just played along bitch, now I'm gonna have to hurt ya."

Goddamn that hurt like a motherfucker! My nose hurt so bad my eyes watered, as blood streamed out of my nose. I tried to crawl away, still feeling stunned but the big guy grabbed my ankle.

"Get off me you fat fuck!" I snarled. I turned and kicked him square in the face. Blood started oozing from the edge of his mouth, and while I knew it wasn't enough of a blow to faze him, it still felt good to get a nice shot in.

"Come here, bitch!"

His eyes were full of rage as he stood back up and shot a creepy grin at me. His mouth was bloody but that seemed to only piss him off. I knew I was a goner if I didn't get away.

He was still between me and the only door out of my apartment. How was I going to get away from this thug?

I struggled to my feet and reached for every ashtray, vase and beer mug decorating my apartment from all kinds of holidays and vacations, throwing each one at the big oaf as I tried to put more distance between us.

"Get! Out!"

Nothing I threw at this guy even slowed him down and I was running out of ashtrays. I chucked a lamp at him in desperation and darted down the hall, locking the bedroom door behind me.

My eyes searched the room. My queen-sized bed sat in the middle with a pink and yellow comforter. On the right was a small pine nightstand a night lamp and to the left a matching chest of drawers. It was a standard two-bedroom apartment, which meant there was no master bathroom, no other means of escape. Just the balcony through the sliding glass door.

I was just about to head for the balcony when I heard a loud crash and saw that he'd kicked my flimsy hollow bedroom door completely off its hinges.

"You fucking bitch, get back here!" His dark eyes glared at me full of anger and hate. Complete terror washed away any confidence I had. My body went limp as he grabbed a fistful of my hair and started dragging me back down the hallway.

The pain was intense as he ripped my hair out by the roots. But I wasn't going down like this. I took a deep breath and started kicking and screaming for help!

"Let me go!"

"We could've done this the easy way, bitch," he hissed, as if I owed him something.

I refused to make it easy for him to snatch me. I squirmed and kicked and screamed, whatever I needed to do to slow him down.

"Help!" I screamed. "Somebody help me! Call 911!"

He grabbed at my mouth and I sank my teeth deep into his hand until I tasted the unmistakable metallic flavor of blood.

"Dumb bitch! Be quiet!" he shouted over me, but I refused to shut up. I continued screaming my head off. I knew my neighbors weren't the type to get involved but they had no problems calling the police for every little peep of noise they deemed too loud.

I screamed, "Help! Help!" as loud as I could, before a heavy crack on the back of my head turned out my lights and everything went black.

Chapter Twenty-Six

Eamon

Tonight would be my last night with Layla. For some fucking reason I was nervous. Sitting inside my living room staring at the roaring fire, I wondered what in the hell the sexy blonde had done to me. I didn't do a lot when it came to women, just a few nights of pleasure and maybe a bauble or two before we'd call it quits. There was no commitment, no relationship, and no chance at anything more.

I liked it like that. No strings attached.

But somehow the girl had gotten under my skin and I wanted more. Goddammit, how in the hell could I possibly want more? What the fuck did *more* even mean? Did I want a relationship? Hell no. But I wasn't ready to let her go yet.

I would eventually, because that was how things worked. I'd always got out before they got that look in their eyes, the one that said they were dreaming of happy endings and white picket fences.

I didn't do any of that shit.

"If she ever fucking gets here!" I stood at the bar and poured more whiskey into a crystal tumbler with one half moon cube of ice and knocked it back like a shot. Layla was already an hour late and it occurred to me that since I'd pissed her off this morning, she might not show up at all. But then I dismissed that thought. Even angry, Layla would honor our agreement if for no other reason than she loved her no good loser of a father.

But still, she wasn't here. Yet, I corrected myself mentally. She'd be here. And when she got here, she'd be all smiles once I let her know her father's debt was officially cleared. She would get that wide, contagious smile on her face, the one that made her look like the sexy girl next door and lean toward me without ever moving forward. Hesitant, because she was as confused by this *thing* going on between us as I was.

Or maybe I was doing exactly what I accused her of doing this morning, dreaming with stars in my eyes? There was a good chance she was late because she didn't want to be here. I didn't believe that though. The way she looked at me, before, during and after sex, spoke of a connection that went beyond the bedroom. That was probably why I'd been such a dick to her earlier.

And now I was paying the price for my behavior.

But I waited impatiently, so sure she wouldn't flake on me tonight. But as another hour passed, my anger turned to worry. Fear. Layla was a woman of her word, of that much I was absolutely fucking certain. Which meant something was wrong.

I picked up the phone and punched in her number, not sure if hearing her voice would leave me relieved or angry. I was saved from that particular answer when the call rang and then straight to voicemail.

"Goddammit!"

Where the fuck was she?

Fuck this. I wouldn't wait one more fucking minute to get to the bottom of this. Either Layla was playing games with me or she was in trouble. Neither option sat well with me, so I grabbed my keys and wallet. If Layla wouldn't come to me, then I'd go to her.

I spent the drive over to her apartment thinking about what I would say to her. If she was home and not deathly ill then I knew my temper would take over but even as I got closer to her place, I knew something wasn't right.

Being raised by Patrick Connelly, I knew how important it was not to ignore gut feelings. Hell, they'd saved my life at least a dozen times over the years, maybe more. Shae and Rourke too. Everything inside me screamed that something was wrong. But when I pulled up to her apartment and saw the lights from outside along with the flickering blue light of the television, I knew that the something wrong was me.

And soon, it would be her too.

I killed the engine and locked the car from my key fob as I walked toward the entrance of Layla's apartment. Heart in my chest, I recognized the feeling as anxiety and brushed it off. I didn't get anxious over women, no matter how good the sex. *Or how sweet the woman,* my subconscious taunted me but I ignored that bastard as well. I was on a mission to get what I wanted.

What I was *owed*, goddammit.

Just as I stepped up to the front door of the lobby and the digital keypad a young couple stepped out, so engrossed with each other they didn't realize I'd slipped in without permission, which was another fact weighing on me as I bypassed the elevator and took the stairs two at a time up to Layla's floor.

It was mostly quiet as I approached her apartment, the low sounds of a television sounded behind me and up ahead the low strains of rock music played. Everything seemed normal. Typical even, and I began to relax. Everything was fine. Layla had probably overslept or she was running behind schedule. That was it.

That was the lie I told myself, anyway.

But when I stood on the cheerful welcome mat in front of her door, a lump lodged in my throat and the whiskey in my gut burned like kerosene.

The door was open just enough for a sliver of light to shine through and I was immediately on alert. It was a damn good thing I didn't go anywhere without at least one piece on me. I slid it out of the holster and nudged the door open with my foot. Leading with my gun, I stepped inside Layla's apartment. It was a complete and total mess.

Pillows and cushions that should have been on the sofa were strewn across the floor and the coffee table was on its side, which left a broken vase with hundreds of little marbles scattered like hail. Glass was everywhere. Whatever had gone down, Layla had put up a fight. Mugs and ashtrays were smashed, along with photo frames, statuettes and even a few porcelain angels were smashed all over the floor. Small droplets of blood had sprayed everything and I bit out a string of fucking expletives.

"Layla! Layla, are you in here?"

There was no answer. If she were here, there would be flashing blue and red lights outside. Layla's blue eyes would be blazing anger the same way they had when she found me pounding her old man's face.

Shit! Layla was in trouble. Sliding my phone from my back pocket, I dialed her number again as I walked around her place, hoping to hear it ring or vibrate somewhere inside. The phone rang in my ear but Layla's apartment remained as silent as ever.

When the voicemail kicked in, I ended the call and dialed the number again. The phone continued to ring with no answer, so I searched Layla's apartment until I found her spare key in a junk drawer in the kitchen. I'd have a talk with her about that but not until I could be sure she was safe. Before I left, I turned off the TV and the lights, sweeping one final glance around the place before locking the door behind me.

Wherever Layla was, I had to fucking find her.

Chapter Twenty-Seven

Layla

Waking up in a strange, dark room was not my idea of a good time, especially when I'd planned to spend the night screaming the name of a hot mobster. But in general, I didn't like waking up with no fucking clue where I was, how I got there, and most of all, who brought me. Oh, and I was tied to a fucking chair.

Luckily a flashing light just outside one of the curtains told me I was at some kind of cheap motel. Based on the stench in the room and the flashing neon lights, it was probably the kind that charged rooms by the hour.

"Hello? Hello?"

Why in the hell did I speak out loud? The room was completely dark, and other than the TV blasting from the rooms on either side of me, there were no other sounds. Was I alone? I thought of the big, sweaty son of a bitch who pushed his way into my apartment.

Was the angry hulk standing behind me, watching and waiting for his opportunity to strike? Or was he just an errand boy and someone worse awaited me? I wondered if Eamon had something to do with this.

Luckily no one answered my call.

I needed to move quickly and quietly, first by figuring out how in the hell to free my hands. I squeezed my eyes shut, tugged as hard as I could, ignoring the pain in my arms as they strained behind me, and waited for the cold metal bite of handcuffs. But it never came. Instead I felt hard plastic dig into my wrists as I jerked to get free.

"Dammit," I hissed. Zip ties. I might not have been the smartest girl on the block, but I knew when zip ties were involved, it was likely a serial killer was around, which meant I was in big damn trouble. I let out a low breath.

Okay think, Layla, think.

I had to find a way out of here. My head throbbed like the world's worst hangover. I blotted that out and squeezed my eyes shut tight until I saw bursts of color like a pain-filled fireworks display. Then slowly, the pain subsided and I snapped my eyes open to focus on the dark room.

By the flashing light outside the window, I could see a chair exactly like mine, a table with a cell phone, and when I twisted just so, I saw behind me at least one bed. I assumed the room had a bathroom, but I couldn't see it. My chair was positioned in the center of the room so all I could see clearly without turning myself into a pretzel was the window and the door.

No doubt trouble waited for me on the other side of the door, but if I could just get to the window, maybe I could escape. I closed my eyes and held my breath, listening for sounds of movement inside and outside the room, anything that said someone was about to hurt me. I heard nothing. Somehow, I managed to get to my feet and stand hunched over with the chair strapped to me. I walked two steps before a wave of pain was back, dizziness crashed over me, and I had to stop. The chair and I slammed back onto the floor, the impact hitting me like a wrecking ball.

I remembered getting hit, but I didn't know what he'd used. A hammer? The butt of a gun? Whatever it was, it made my head throb like a jackhammer. Making all that worse, I couldn't seem to stand more than a few seconds before my legs turned to limp noodles.

Okay Layla, get up and do this.

I sucked in several deep breaths and let them out slowly before I stood up again and moved another few feet toward the window before I collapsed to the floor again. As soon as my ass hit the seat, the doorknob turned and seconds later the thug appeared in the doorway.

"Fuck," I whispered.

The big fat ginger grinned. "Unfortunately that's not on the menu. Yet. But you are a pretty little thing."

I bit back a shudder. This guy had already shown a love of violence.

I snarled, "Why am I here?"

It didn't take a genius to figure out that one of the two men in my life right now had to be involved somehow. *If I could get my hands on Eamon or Dad right now!*

"Don't worry Layla," he grunted. "I have no plans to hurt you."

He stepped inside the room and walked over to my chair. Up close, I could smell the sweat, beer and stale cigarette stench coming from him. He traced a finger down my jawline, and I thought I would gag, recoiling out of his reach.

"You already hurt me or is beating up on women some kind of sick foreplay to you?"

He shrugged and took a step back, pulling a pack of cigarettes from his pocket. He popped one in his mouth in that practiced way of a lifelong smoker.

"You had to be difficult."

"Right. And when strangers come up to your door blowing stinky smoke in your face, you just let them in, right?"

This guy was full of shit but everything about him said low-level gangster. I'd seen enough movies to spot one and this guy was nowhere near as polished as Eamon, which meant he wasn't on the same level. At least I assumed so. Then again, I was new to the mobster world and maybe the movies had gotten it wrong all these years.

"Doesn't matter." He lit the cigarette and took a long satisfying pull before blowing all the smoke in my face.

"Asshole."

"You're here now," he said, like I hadn't said a word. "You won't get hurt as long as you behave."

I could just imagine what he meant by *behave*.

"What the fuck is going on? Tell me why I'm here!"

"You've got fire. I can see why he likes you."

"He? He who? Who the fuck is *he*?" I wanted to know but I was as terrified as I was curious, and terror won out. "Are you going to kill me?"

He smiled behind his scruff. "Not if I don't have to."

Which wasn't exactly a definitive answer, was it? I could only glare at the jerk who seemed to be having a lot of fun at my expense.

"What does that mean?" I wished I didn't sound so scared. I knew that put me at a disadvantage.

"You're leverage and that's all you need to know. Now be a good girl and I won't have to hurt you. No matter how much I might want to."

This time, the thug ignored my attempts to outrun the brush of his hand down my cheek, his smelly hand making me retch.

A phone rang and the ringtone sounded oddly familiar. The guy lifted a phone off of the table and held it up to give me a good look at it.

"Hey," I said, more outraged now than scared. "That's my phone!"

He grunted again, this time into the phone. "Hello?"

His face tugged into a smile that shaved about ten years from his haggard face. He laughed just a little too loud and too fake.

"It's good to hear from you too, Connelly."

Connelly? Eamon? That answered the question to which man was responsible for my current dilemma. This night really hadn't gone how I planned.

No, not at all.

Chapter Twenty-Eight

Eamon

I tried her phone one last time and finally someone picked up.

But it wasn't Layla.

I fucking knew that voice. And it pissed me off that he was the one answering Layla's phone.

"What are you doing with Layla's phone? What the fuck do you want, Rico?"

He gave me a deep chuckle that made me want to pound his face, and next, the fucker gave me click of his tongue.

"Where are your manners, Connelly? None of this is personal, you know that. It's just business."

Yeah, I knew it. But assholes like Rico took great pleasure in their work, which always made it personal.

"You got my attention," I said, anger boiling in my veins.

Not even Rico was good enough to break through my fortress of security, and even if he did, he'd be dead before he ever got close enough to me to make a move.

"Good. Because my client wanted me to make sure you were paying attention."

Another deep chuckle sounded, and my jaws clenched with the effort of holding back my words.

"Right. Who exactly is this client?"

Though I could probably guess who was behind this, hearing it straight from a professional hit man would be all the evidence I needed to fuck up the lives of everyone involved. Including Rico.

"We both know who. Don't be cute," Rico grumbled.

"That's a gift of genetics and I can't help it."

I knew that would get under his skin because he was damn sensitive about his ugly mug.

"I might know who your client is, but if you don't confirm, I might be afraid of the wrong people."

That pulled another laugh from him. "The Milano family."

The name came out on a frustrated groan.

"And what do they want with Layla? She has nothing to do with either their business or mine."

"Maybe not, but she *is* involved with you and that's a damn sight better than being in the business."

A simple enough conclusion to draw, one that meant they were watching me. Watching both of us.

"Explain."

"You two are sweet together. Really, you are." His sigh came heavy down the line. "I saw you two this morning and that slow, lingering kiss. A couple in love if I ever saw one."

"You're wrong, Rico. What you saw was me saying goodbye to a piece of ass. Nothing more."

The words turned sour on my tongue but I had to say them. I had to make Rico think Layla didn't mean anything to me. "You've got bad intel."

"Is that right?"

Rico's gruff voice sounded amused but I wasn't fooled. He looked like a sloppy bastard and smelled even worse, but nobody did contract wet work like Rico.

"Yep."

"Then why are you calling her?"

I laughed. "Because we had plans tonight. Naked plans and I was in the mood to get my dick wet, something you wouldn't know about since you haven't seen your dick since the nineties."

Rico laughed. "If she ain't yours then I guess I'll stick my dick in her."

"Get away from me you stinky bastard!" I heard Layla's voice ring out in the distance. "No, don't touch me!"

As hard as it was, I said nothing. Any clue, any inkling that Layla was more than a quick fuck and she'd be everything Rico and the Milano family hoped for.

Rico came back on the line with a laugh. "She's feisty, Connelly. I can see why you like her."

"Are we done?"

"Yeah, we're done," he said easily. Too easily.

Layla's screams grew more terrified. "Get your greasy paws off me!" I had to close my mind to what he was doing to her or I wouldn't be able to get control of this situation. I had to stay focused.

"Just listen to this," he snarled into the phone, "and then we're done."

I closed my eyes as Layla yelled and fought with Rico, the sounds getting louder as he moved closer to her. A loud smack sounded and another cry from Layla. "Ow!" That was it, one short sharp scream followed by small continuous whimpering.

I gripped the phone so hard I thought it might break, but it was the only thing keeping me from threatening to rip that asshole limb from limb. If I said one word, if I gave him any indication that Layla was more than a fuck buddy, he'd do more than smack her around. Those Milano fuckers would guarantee it.

"None of that means a damn thing to me if you don't tell me what you expect of me."

"That's easy. Meet me tonight. The Kinky Elephant. Eleven o'clock."

The call ended abruptly and as bad as I wanted to throw the phone across Layla's parking lot, I held my temper.

"Goddammit!" I screamed into the night.

I knew exactly what I had to do, and I needed my family at my side.

Chapter Twenty-Nine

Layla

There were times in people's lives when they looked around and wondered how in the hell they ended up where they were. I was having one of those moments as I sat and listened to Eamon tell the greasy pig just how little I meant to him. The answer was very fucking little. So little, it might as well be nothing at all.

And Eamon was my only hope.

Yeah, I wondered how I got here when just last week I thought the mob was something that used to happen back in the nineties. I thought they only existed for the sake of the bad guys you love to hate on every crime drama show that aired during primetime. But now, I knew the truth. The mob wasn't just real, they were alive and well in Rocket, Nevada. What were the odds?

And I was somehow caught in the middle of a mob war. Or at least I assumed the Milanos the greasy ginger had mentioned were also a mob family because, why the hell not? *Just fuck my life right now.*

"He called you a piece of ass. Pretty cold if you ask me."

"Yeah, well I didn't ask, did I?"

And I didn't want to hear his fucking views on the world.

"Still, if some chick I was clearly into said that about me, I'd be pretty pissed off."

In an effort to intimidate me, I guessed, he pulled out three different guns, one from his ankle, his waistband and one holstered by his ribs. Then, as calmly as you please, he sat at a table by the window and began to clean them.

I snorted at him. "Then you have a higher opinion of women than I do of men because nothing any of you motherfuckers do can ever surprise me."

The latest shock was Dad and his secret life that involved the mob or the mafia—what was the difference anyway?

"Really?" He snorted his disbelief. "Because I saw you two this morning outside your apartment and to me, you looked like two people falling in love."

"Like you know what love is."

He frowned and took a break from cleaning his guns. "Don't judge me by my work. We all have to make a living lady."

Who was this guy kidding? I rolled my eyes and leaned back, trying to get comfortable tied to a chair with my head throbbing along with my cheek.

"I'm sorry Mr. Kidnapper and Abuser of Women. Please tell me your philosophies on love."

He smiled again. "I like you, blondie. And I will tell you because you need to hear it."

"Really, I don't. Love isn't my thing."

"Bullshit."

The grin he wore took the sting off his words. "I saw you two this morning, and I heard the way he clenched his teeth over the phone, hard enough to turn them to dust. And if you really didn't mean a thing to him, he woulda hung up right away."

What the hell had happened to my life that I was taking relationship advice from a thug cleaning his guns while I was tied to a chair?

"Why bother giving me false hope if you're only going to kill me?"

I was done with talking to this asshole. I was done with talking period. I turned my head away from him and stared at a crack in the wall, wondering how many other people had been tied to chairs here. How many other people had stared at that crack without realizing it was the last thing they'd ever see?

"Don't ignore me, Layla."

"Stop saying my name like you know me. You don't."

"Oh, but I do." He grinned and went back to his guns. "You think you're gonna be the woman who changes Eamon."

"Wrong."

"I've seen plenty of women like you over the years," he said again and shook his head. "Guys like him don't change."

"Good, because I'm not trying to change anyone." It wasn't my job to change anyone, least of all someone so entrenched in this life. He was who he was, and I fell for him anyway, dummy that I was.

"You don't strike me as a good time girl."

"I'm not," I told him angrily because there was no way in hell I would tell him what I was actually doing with Eamon. "But I am a sucker for a beautiful man so I figured a guy like Eamon was perfect."

"Why's that?"

"Because my heart was never in any danger with a player like him."

If only I realized that a lot sooner.

"If you say so." Bright red eyebrows arched in disbelief and I shrugged.

"I don't need you to believe me, not when I'll be dead soon anyway." There, I'd said it out loud, the thing I feared the most. The thing that was looking more and more inevitable and I'd just blurted it out like an idiot.

"I might not kill you."

I didn't bother looking at him because I knew he was lying. I just wondered if he'd kill me before or after Eamon showed up.

Chapter Thirty

Eamon

Patrick sat in his usual spot behind his desk with his hands folded neatly, his eyes inscrutable. "And how exactly do you know this girl, son?" he asked me.

I nodded at him to buy some time as I gathered my thoughts. Shae, Rourke and Patrick all looked at me expectantly. "She is someone I spend time with on occasion."

It wasn't the whole truth and the skeptical look on Patrick's face said he knew it.

"She's also the daughter of Peter Michaels." I added.

"Goddammit Eamon!" My father shouted, slapping his hand on his desk. "Jesus, Mary and Joseph, when will you ever learn?"

"I know, I know. But she has nothing to do with the business. Hell, she's not even my girlfriend." I knew

I had to walk a fine line between downplaying our relationship while also encouraging the family to help me save her.

Rourke pushed off the wall and stood beside me with both arms crossed over his chest. "If she's not special to you, why are we even talking about her?"

Shae glared at our cousin, who had a lot more of Patrick in him than anyone wanted to admit. "I can't believe you just said that shit. You want to let an innocent woman die for what, to show the fucking Milanos that we're not afraid of them?"

Shae shook his head, anger transforming his boyish features to the man he was on his way to becoming. "Fuck that noise. We ought to take this opportunity to end those motherfuckers once and for all."

Patrick rocked slowly in his chair, his movements as deliberate as his silence. "I agree with Shae but we have to be smart. This is the perfect opportunity to make an example of them."

I agreed, but all I could think about was Layla getting caught up in the middle of our shit.

"That's great but they're not taking Layla to The Kinky Elephant, which is where I'm supposed to meet Rico."

"You're not showing up for that meeting." Patrick's expression was ruthless, and I didn't argue.

"We need to find out where they're keeping the girl," Rourke offered quietly. "If we get her while they're waiting on you, then we get the advantage. They'll still think they have leverage, but we'll know better."

Patrick grinned his proud grin and nodded. "Exactly. How do we find out where she is?"

Shae leaned over and held his hand out to me. "Give me your phone. I have a guy who can do this for us."

"You do? Since when does my kid brother have connections I know nothing about?"

"Hell, yeah. Can't run an organization like ours without a couple tech geniuses in the back pocket." I handed him the phone with a heavy sigh.

"We'll have a hit on her location in less than five minutes," Shae said and left the room with a whistle.

"It makes me happy to see you three boys working as a team," Patrick said, cracking the first warm smile of the meeting. "It's my greatest dream for the future of this family."

His gaze swung from me to Rourke and back to me. "In the future Eamon, keep a closer eye on your women."

"Who in the hell knew the Milanos were ready to make a move? Last I heard, they'd just set up a few gaming lounges. Recently."

"You should always expect a little cockroach to try and become a bigger cockroach by taking out the biggest of the bunch. It is the nature of cockroaches. They want more than they deserve. More than they are capable of handling."

Rourke nodded his agreement. "This has the younger Milanos written all over it, Uncle. They took his woman ..."

"Not my woman," I corrected unnecessarily because Rourke ignored me.

"And they didn't even ask for terms other than a meeting. Fucking amateurs."

"It doesn't matter which Milano the threat comes from," Patrick assured us. "Now they will all pay for their hubris."

Shae strode back in with a shit-eating grin on his face. "Good news. Your girl or at least her phone is at a shitty by the hour motel about two miles away from The Kinky Elephant."

"That was fast," Patrick commented, sounding impressed with his youngest boy.

"The dumbass left the phone on, which made our job easy as hell. We need to keep your phone on Eamon, so we can check in to make sure it's not on the move."

I snapped my head and looked around the room at my family. The three men closest to me who hadn't hesitated to jump in and help me play the hero.

"Got it. Now, does anyone have any ideas how we get these bastards?"

Patrick cleared his throat and we all turned to him. "The goal here is two-fold. We get the girl first and then we end the Milano family. We *end* them," he reiterated. "Got it?"

"Got it," we all said at the same time

"Good. Now I expect you three to come up with a plan to save the girl and put this Milano headache to rest."

Patrick's heavy gaze landed on each of us, the weight of his expectation heavy on our shoulders. "Come back when you have a plan that can work."

We had our orders and left Patrick alone in his office and ended up in our favorite room in the house, the game room, to plan. We all headed straight for the felt-covered pool table, where I racked the balls while

Rourke and Shae prepared their sticks. It had been the same since we were kids who didn't have the strength to put a ball into a pocket.

Shae spoke up first. "Hear me out before you say no," he said with caution. Before saying anything else, he bent over the pool table and hit the cue ball with a deafening crack. "I'll go in and get, what's her name?"

"Layla," I offered reluctantly because the thought of anyone else putting their hands on Layla, rescuing her, left a bad taste in my mouth.

"Right. I'll go in and get Layla while E-money meets with Rico as though nothing is wrong. We'll have a few guys in place as backup for you because there is no fucking way in hell there won't be a Milano or two hanging around."

I glanced at my watch. Ten fifteen, which meant we had a little more than an hour to get our shit together. Rourke sighed. "And what the hell am I supposed to do, Shae? Stay here and work on some spreadsheets?"

Shae barked out a laugh and easily sank his final green ball and then the black one before he rolled his pool stick onto the table and crossed his arms. "Not unless you have some quarterly reports or some shit to take care of. I was thinking you'd be our logistics guy. Watch the motel from a strategic angle and let us know what's going on so we can act accordingly."

"Shit, that's brilliant," I said. Relief poured out of me in a loud exhale. "Let's work it out now and then take it to Patrick." With a plan in place, my anxiety had abated. Some.

Chapter Thirty-One

Layla

Considering that I'd been kidnapped, tied to a chair, and beaten, I felt surprisingly calm. Fearless almost, in fact. Maybe it was because I'd spent the past hour thinking about my own mortality, about how much lower Dad would sink once I was gone. About the fact that I'd be dead in the morning and by evening Eamon would likely have someone else sucking his dick.

Neither thought was very helpful as I sat alone in the dark motel room, but as far as I'd come in my life, it turned out, I was no different than generations of women who cared about the men in their lives more than they did about themselves.

It was a pathetic thing to figure out about myself when I had less than an hour to live, but at least I wouldn't die lying to myself.

The knob on the outside door turned and I dropped my head so it hung limp like I was sleeping. If the sweaty goon meant to do more than kill me, I'd have to catch him by surprise if I stood a chance in hell of getting out of this mess alive. A chance that grew slimmer by the minute.

"Wake up!" he barked.

I stayed where I was, slowly counting to four on every inhale and exhale to mimic the deep breathing associated with being asleep.

"Hey, I said wake up!"

He kicked my chair and I couldn't stop the gasp that escaped at the impact.

Another laugh sounded, from a new voice.

"Damn, that Eamon Connelly has excellent taste in women, she is one fine piece of ass."

"Hands off, Angelo. Remember Lorenzo's orders."

"Chill, Rico. I'm just having a little fun. You havin' fun sweetheart?"

The other guy sounded slick and arrogant, like someone who rarely had to face the consequences of his action.

"I'm talking to you, bitch," he said and his voice filled me with revulsion.

"There's only one bitch in here and I'm looking right at him." Okay, it wasn't my smartest move but at that point I didn't have much to lose anyway.

The other man, Angelo, lunged forward but the sweaty guy, Rico, grabbed at him and his thick black hair fell over one eye.

"Just give me five minutes alone with this bitch, Rico. Five minutes and I'll teach her how she's supposed to talk to a man."

I snorted a laugh. "If you find any men let me know." Okay, now I'd gone batshit nuts.

Angelo slipped free of Rico's sweaty grasp, raised his hand and lowered a backhand on the same damn cheek Rico had hit earlier. It hurt like a son of a bitch but I only let out a small groan, refusing to give him the satisfaction.

"Good thing you're wearing your mother's best jewelry or I might have thought it was a bitch hitting me."

He lunged again but Rico stepped between us, which I was grateful for since a small stream of blood trickled down the side of my throbbing face.

"Cool it, Angelo," Rico hissed, "or I'll knock you the fuck out."

"Yeah on whose authority?"

Rico's shoulders straightened and he spit out, "Lorenzo's. He has a plan so don't fuck it up. Or do and you'll be the one paying the price, not me."

The phone in Rico's hand, my phone, rang, startling us all. But it ended the fight when Angelo snatched it away.

"Eamon Connelly, what a surprise."

Eamon? Why was he calling when he was supposed to show up in twenty or thirty minutes? The answer stared me right in the face even as I refused to believe it. He wasn't coming and I was definitely going to die tonight.

My eyes were glued to Angelo's frowning face in search of any information I could get about my fate.

"What the fuck do you mean you're not coming? You don't show up and your bitch is dead."

Whatever he said, I couldn't hear and for that much I was glad.

"No, meet us at The Kinky Elephant."

The rest of the conversation was lost to me and I hadn't decided if it was good or bad when Angelo tossed my phone across the room.

"That motherfucker! If he thinks he can disrespect me and my family, he's got another fucking thing coming!"

"Think."

Angelo glared at me. "What the fuck did you just say to me, bitch?"

"I said *think*. The phrase is 'another think coming', not another thing, Einstein."

He lunged again and Rico was there once again.

"Enough, Angelo! What did he say?"

"The fucker said he wasn't coming. That he'd catch up with you another time."

Angelo peeked around Rico and grinned. "Too bad for you sweetheart, because I've got serious plans for that hot little body."

"Fuck!" Rico said and he began to pace, acting as a barrier between me and Angelo the psychopath.

"We'll just have to dump her body, bloody and beaten, on his fucking doorstep," Angelo suggested with a disgusting sneer.

"No. He's coming, I know it." Rico stopped pacing and looked from me to Angelo. "He's coming here."

Eamon was coming here? For me?

Angelo laughed. "Even better. With all the men we have, he'll be dead before he even makes it to the door. You weren't dumb enough to tell him where you are, were you?"

Rico gave him a dirty look. "I'm not the fuckup here, Angelo so no, I didn't tell him a goddamn thing."

"Then why are you so sure he's coming here?"

Angelo's expression went from laughing and carefree to deadly serious. "You're not trying to screw over my family are you? Because you know what we do to rats."

"I don't owe your family a fucking thing, Angelo. You pay for a service and I provide it. Letting you and your fucking nephew tag along wasn't part of the deal, so next time you threaten me, I'll drive a nail through both of your fucking eyes."

A long tense moment passed between the men, a silent pissing contest where Rico seemed to emerge as the winner.

"Whatever," Angelo grumbled and stormed out of the motel room, slamming the door behind him.

Rico let out a sigh and turned to face me, pointing a big meaty finger at my face. "Don't try to kick or bite me. I won't kill you but I *will* make you hurt. Got it?"

I nodded, my mouth instantly dry.

"Good."

When Rico stepped behind me and hoisted me and the chair in the air, I took the opportunity to look around the room in search of a weapon or another escape. My gaze fell on a plain white shower curtain. So I'd found the bathroom.

"Kind of hard to go to the bathroom with my arms tied to the chair."

Rico grunted a laugh. "If you have to piss, hold it or don't, but you're not getting out of that chair."

He gave me one last angry look, turned out the light and slammed the door behind him.

A second too late I found my voice. "Hey! Where are you going? You can't leave me in..." the sound of another door opening and shutting, taking the last of my hope with it. "... *here.*"

Then I heard voices outside. Male voices. Talking so quietly I couldn't make out the words.

Wait. What was that? A window sliding open? A startled gasp flew out of me, because Rico had left me in darkness. What now? Or more likely, who now? I wanted to call out for help, but fear had lodged in my throat and stopped me. What if Angelo had decided he didn't care what Rico's orders were and had come back for me? I decided to stay as quiet as possible, trying to hear what was happening.

I held my breath, listening carefully as wood scraped against wood and the bathroom window opened, letting more night sounds inside.

Then a grunt, along with a crashing noise came from behind the closed shower curtain, and I sucked in a silent scream and waited for my fate to unfold.

Chapter Thirty-Two

Eamon

"All right guys, Rico just exited room 119. Bottom floor, corner room." Rourke's voice rang out clear and crisp in my ear piece, doing fuck all to calm my nerves.

There was no reason for nerves anyway. I'd done shit like this a million times before. It usually came easy to me, but even I could admit that normally I didn't give a shit what happened to anyone without the Connelly name. But this was different. As much as I wanted to fool myself that Layla was nothing more than casual sex and intense orgasms, it was a fucking lie. I wanted her. Bad. Bad enough to enlist my family to help save her fucking life.

Shit, I might be falling for this chick.

"I'm at the window. It's unlocked." Shae sounded cool and calm with a hint of pleasure to his voice.

"Too fucking easy," he whispered while Rourke and I listened for any signs of distress. "Okay, I'm inside."

"Is she in there?"

"She's not in the shower which is where I currently am so give me a damn min—"

The line went silent and panic rose up in my gut.

"Shae, you there? Answer me, dammit."

Several long seconds passed before he spoke again.

"Sorry. I heard something in the bathroom and it turned out to be Layla."

"You barged in on her in the bathroom?"

He laughed. "No, she's tied to a chair. Gotta go guys, kick some ass while I save the damsel in distress."

His connection went dead and though I should have felt relief, more anxiety welled up in me.

"Relax bro, she'll be fine. Your head in the game?"

I took a deep breath and glanced at my reflection in the rearview mirror, giving me something I rarely needed. A mental pep talk.

"Yeah, my head's in the game Rourke."

"Good, because we got movement on the east side of the motel. Two guys, both armed. They don't look like Milano's men."

Shit. "Colors?"

"Yeah. Purple and black." Rourke's matter of fact tone concealed his emotions, a fact that normally pissed me off but today it was comforting. Those colors belonged to the Purple Aces, a group of crazy fuckers with ambitions of being Somebody with a capital 'S.'

"Any Milano muscle around?"

From my spot at the diner across the street I couldn't see anyone so I stepped from the car.

"Not yet but you have an audience."

My head immediately began to swivel in all directions, checking out all the angles danger could come from. Mostly I got darkness. Not helpful.

"Good, I always wanted to star in my own show."

Rourke's chuckle sounded down the line. "Rico is at your one o'clock."

I spotted that big fucker because there was no amount of darkness that could shield his girth. "Got it."

I crossed the street, my eyes moving constantly, keeping a close eye on Rico while looking out for any of Lorenzo's boys.

Rico locked in on me as I approached. He had a gun in his right hand. I smiled and pointed at his fat belly.

"Rico. Good to see you. You lost weight?"

"Fuck you, Connelly."

A laugh escaped me even though I wasn't feeling jolly, and I took a step forward. "You're not my type, Rico."

"That's far enough," he said, but I heard the wariness creep into his tone, so I took another step forward.

I knew talk of Layla would get him to lower his guard, at least a little. "Where's the girl?" I said.

He shrugged. "Keep your hand away from that gun stuffed in your pants and maybe I'll tell you."

"Why would I do a stupid thing like that?"

A few more steps forward and I heard two sets of footsteps a few paces behind me.

"So the pussies behind me can try and get the jump on me? Try again, Rico."

He raised the gun and aimed it at me, and I could see his hands trembling. I had him right where I wanted him. "Toss that piece nice and slow over this way, Rico."

"Fuck you."

Rico threw his head back and laughed, a sliver of pale white fat around his belly shone under the yellowish security lights provided by the cheap motel.

"Nah, I got a curvy blonde inside with more than enough holes for me and the boys."

My fingers twitched with the urge to lay that fat fuck out, but I couldn't do shit until Shae gave me the all clear. So I just smiled.

"Then I guess I got here just in time for the party. You might want to lower that gun before it falls out of your hand or you shoot one of these motherfuckers coming up behind me by mistake. The last thing you need is to have to explain to the boss man how you lost the girl and shot his men."

I took a step back and turned toward the two men who'd stopped about twenty feet away in front of motel room. I figured Layla was in the room behind them.

"Take one more step Connelly, and I'll put two bullets in that bitch before you make your way out of the parking lot."

A broad smile crossed my face. Damn, I loved it when a plan worked out so beautifully. Even Jesus himself couldn't have planned this shit better.

"Angelo Milano, I thought that was the stench of rotten garbage I smelled." I turned back to him and slid my piece out of my waistband, finger hovering half an inch off the trigger. "Lorenzo must not be too serious if you're the one he sent."

"Fuck you, Connelly. Soon your family will be nothing but a memory in this town."

I laughed. "Is this your version of a 'Rocket ain't big enough for the both of us' speech? It was better in High Noon."

"Laugh it up, pretty boy."

Shae's breathless voice sounded in my ear. "E-dogg, I got her."

And just like that, everything was fine again. The edges of my vision cleared and my pulse slowed until everything was in absolute fucking focus.

"Backup is in place," Rourke confirmed, and I was ready.

"You know why I'm laughing, Angelo? Because you're a fucking joke. Your whole fucking family is a goddamn joke. You think you can come in here and take what belongs to *my* family? Well then motherfucker, you better be prepared to fight for it." While I talked I took a few more steps forward, taunting them both.

Angelo laughed. "You wanna go at it right here in the parking lot like a bunch of teenagers? It ain't my style, but I'm down."

"And that's the problem with you Milanos, small brains equal small thoughts. You want what I got, you better be willing to fucking take it."

Angelo, pussy that he was, took a step back and bumped into the door. "You want me to take it?"

"You don't have the balls."

"You want me to take what's yours?" His voice grew louder, more agitated by the second.

"I want you to try so I can take my time killing you." Then, I let my face relax into a smile.

"Something funny?"

I shrugged. "Besides your face?"

Angelo was good and pissed off, taking another step back and grabbing the doorknob. He twisted it and looked over his shoulder with a smile. "Killing her won't mean shit to me. Can you say the same?"

"Whatever happens next Angelo, just know that you brought it all on yourself." Another wave of deep calm washed over me and it was almost as if I could see the next few minutes unfold. That comforting thought put my feet on the move, right toward Angelo Milano.

Chapter Thirty-Three

Layla

"Layla, I presume?"

A handsome man who looked like a younger version of Eamon smiled down at me but I was still on alert.

"Who are you?"

Just because he looked like Eamon didn't mean he was any relation to him and for all I knew he could've been part of the crew that came with Angelo and Rico.

The man switched his gun to his left hand and stuck out his right. "Shae Connelly. Your savior."

"Eamon's younger brother." That was a relief at least. "I'd love to shake your hands but I'm zip tied to this damn chair."

He flashed a boyish grin and holstered his gun before pulling a knife from a back pocket. Shae leaned over, his masculine scent invaded my nostrils and it was a damn sight better than the stench of Rico that still lingered. He slid the knife between my wrists in an upward motion and my upper body fell forward.

"Now you're free," he announced.

"Thanks," I said, a little lightheaded from swinging from death's door to rescue. My arms and hands tingled as I shook them out and feeling returned. But when I tried to stand, I said, "Oh shit!"

Shae reached for me as I fell forward. "I gotcha. How are your window climbing skills?"

I looked up at his smiling face and groaned. "Nonexistent, but my survival instincts run pretty damn deep."

And I realized that in a few minutes, hopefully less, we would be free. I would be free.

"Wait!" I said as panic set in once again. "They're setting up a trap. There's the guy Rico but also another guy named Angelo. They talked about *the others* and made it sound like they planned on killing Eamon."

It wasn't something I wanted to think about but seeing as he'd come to my rescue it was the least I could do.

"We figured that out, but thanks. Don't worry, it's being taken care of, sweetheart."

"What does that mean?"

"It means that it and they are being taken care of. Don't worry. But we really need to get the hell out of here. Now."

"Right. Lead the way."

I was ready to get out of this damn motel and jump into a hot bath with a big bottle of tequila. This had been a tequila kind of week and red wine just wouldn't cut it.

"You first."

I wanted to argue but the voices outside grew louder and I knew we didn't have much time. Stepping inside the shower, my heart began to beat faster but I sucked in two big breaths and let them out slowly before I peeked outside the window and then back at Shae. "Just jump on top of the dumpster?"

"Yep. It's only about five feet."

"Okay." I could do this. Out the window was the path to freedom and there was no reason to hesitate. None at all.

"Just jump, Layla."

"Right. Just jump." I repeated the words more to strengthen my resolve than anything else.

And then, I jumped.

Chapter Thirty-Four

Eamon

"Shoot goddammit! I said shoot!" Rico stood between me and Angelo. The sniveling piece of shit cowered back there like a child hiding from the boogeyman, yelling at the Purple Aces to shoot at me. I couldn't believe Rico was the best hitman in Rocket. The family had even used him before. Now, he was just a big idiot.

"What the fuck?" Rico asked. He looked around at the group of men decked out in purple and black, bewildered. Terrified. Trapped.

"What did they promise you, Rico?" I called out.

Rico frowned. "What the fuck are you talking about?" We both knew he was lying.

"Lorenzo, or was it Angelo? What did they offer you to put your life at risk?"

He scoffed but I saw the beads of sweat forming on his forehead and his neck, the dark stains all over his shirt.

"My life is always at risk."

"Bullshit. You're a hired assassin, the risk is minimal. Did Angelo promise to make you a made man if you snatched Layla? Did Lorenzo promise you guaranteed work?"

"What business is it of yours?"

"That's what happens when you deal with amateurs like the Milano family. Money is the universal language and we have more of it than the Milanos. Hell, we have more to offer a gang on the rise like the Purple Aces. And unfortunately for you..." I waited a beat, savoring the look of abject horror on Angelo's face. "They accepted."

"Bullshit," he spat from around Rico's shoulder. "You're lying."

"He's not." Street was the current leader of the Aces and the man had one goal, to make a shit ton of money. A trait I could relate to. "It's not personal, ya know, just business."

"Motherfucker!" Angelo panicked, hand still wrapped around the doorknob of the hotel room, he somehow still managed to fumble it, giving me even more time to gain on him.

"Are you running, Angelo? I heard you were the crazy one. The unstable one." Mostly he was cruel, the product of being raised by a sadist like Lorenzo.

"That's a disappointment. I was hoping we could have a little fun."

His eyes widened in terror and finally the door opened and sent both Rico and Angelo falling backwards into the room, Rico now splayed out on top of Angelo.

"You're the crazy one!" he said, his voice rising in a frenzy of fear.

"Yeah and you're just a spoiled prick who made a deadly mistake."

My footsteps were slow and deliberate, an even slower smile spread across my face as he tried to get Rico's fat ass off his legs.

"Fuck you, Connelly. You can't kill me."

He was so certain, so fucking sure that the rules he saw on some episode of *Mob Wives* were the rules we operated by in real life that I almost felt sorry for the asshole. Almost.

"Yeah, according to who?"

He finally broke free of Rico's torso and slid against the filthy blue-gray carpet on his ass.

"Lorenzo."

I laughed as I crossed the threshold, standing beside Rico's panting, sweaty body. "Was that his way of getting you to go on this fool's errand or are you acting on your own?"

I looked down at Rico and his eyes slammed into mine with a look of resignation. One I respected but when he started this life, he knew this was likely how it was gonna end. He closed his eyes and I raised my gun and pulled the trigger. Twice.

"Not that it matters."

"Oh shit! Fuck!"

"Calm down, you've cleaned up worse in the family biz, right?"

Stepping over Rico's lifeless body, I took a few more steps forward.

"I wonder if I'll get a discount on this job since you're family and all."

That had Angelo scrambling to his feet. He scanned the room and I knew just what he was looking for, or who.

"Where ...?"

His eyes went wide and he darted to the bathroom with me three steps behind him because I didn't want to miss when he found the bathroom empty.

"No!"

"Oh yeah," I said unnecessarily as he stared at the turned over chair and the white zip ties still dangling from the arm.

"No! Goddammit." He looked to the open window and ran to it, looking left and then right. "No! No! No!"

That sound, the panic and the fear, it all made me smile.

"Angelo."

He froze and slowly slid down into the tub with the long vein of rust through it until he landed on his feet. Angelo stood slowly. Too fucking slowly for him to do anything but go for his piece, if the dumb fuck even carried one.

"You should've shot me when you had the chance."

Slowly he lifted his gun from his side like this was a goddamn movie shoot. I lifted my gun and shot him in the thigh. I enjoyed the sight of his leg giving out under him more than a God-fearing man should have, but I didn't fear God. I respected his wrath, but I feared no man.

"I think that's my line."

Angelo's chest rose and fell quickly, his breathing shallow from the pain, his brow slick with sweat.

"You know what this means, right?"

I nodded. "That whether you live or die is up to me?"

"This," he panted, his breathing labored. "Means. War."

The dumb shit smiled like he'd be around to see if his prediction proved true.

"Don't kill him," Rourke warned in my ear.

I frowned even though he couldn't see me. "End them, he said. End. Them."

Rourke sighed. "He changed his mind. Uncle now wants a slow, painful death."

I shrugged. "I'm fine with that." Angelo flinched when I dropped down to my knees and stuck my thumb in the hole in his thigh. "Must be your lucky day, Angelo. You get to live."

"Ah fuck! Stop!"

"But by the time tomorrow comes, you'll wish you were dead."

Applying just a few more pounds of pressure produced a scream that spoke of his agony and that anguish stretched a smile across my face.

"B-B-But I won't be," he barely stammered out.

I'd get busy making sure he'd regret seeing the sun every fucking morning for the rest of his life. "If I see any Milano anywhere in Rocket and it doesn't involve cleaning up a bunch of dead gangbangers, you're the first one I'll kill. Only I'll do it real slow this time while I make your father and brother watch."

When Angelo finally passed out from the pain, I grabbed his phone to make sure he didn't make a liar out of me.

As soon as I stepped back over Rico's body and outside the room, I sucked in a deep breath and let it out. "Where is she?"

Rourke chuckled. "Insisted on waiting by that ugly ass car of yours."

My feet carried me in the direction of my car, my legs moving faster and faster, needing to see for myself that she really was okay.

My car came into sight seconds later and then Layla, looking sexy and disheveled and a little worse for wear in jeans, a black top and no shoes.

"Layla."

Her smile spread slowly, shyly as she took me in with heat in her eyes. But it wasn't the heat that had my walk increasing to a jog, it was the way the bottom of her smile quivered.

"Eamon," she said and broke off in a sob.

In seconds I had Layla in my arms, holding her close. Holding her tight.

"Oh babe, I'm so fucking sorry." Her body felt frail as it shook from her sobs. I hoped my body, my warmth and my presence offered her some comfort.

"You're safe now, Layla. You're safe."

She pulled back and looked up at me, cupping my jaw so gently I leaned in before I thought better of it. Her green eyes glowed in the moonlight. "Thank you, Eamon."

Goddamn, this woman had the power to completely undo me. I knew what it was I felt for her, what I had been reluctant to put a name to until the moment I had her in my arms. Love. That's what it was. And as soon as she was ready to hear it, I would tell her.

"Don't thank me, Layla. I couldn't have left you here for anything in the world."

Her smile trembled with unshed tears. "I know my timing sucks," she began and sucked in a breath, "but I was planning on telling you tonight or last night and then everything went straight to hell. And I want—"

"Layla," I blurted out to stop her nervous chatter.

She blinked, smiled, took a deep breath. "I'm falling in love with you and I want to see you past tonight."

"Signing off," Rourke said quickly.

"Not me, I'm not missing this," Shae said with a smile in his voice.

I didn't need my brother around when I finally claimed Layla, body and soul, so I grabbed the device out of my ear, took her hand and helped her inside the car.

"Let's get out of here."

"That sounds perfect."

Chapter Thirty-Five

Layla

What in the hell was I thinking, blurting it out like that? He looked terrified. Actually that wasn't true, he didn't have time to look *anything* before he started grumbling to himself about nosy brothers. In fact, he hadn't said one damn word to me since we got in his car. After a thirty- minute ride, and we'd been at his house for another thirty minutes.

In absolute fucking silence. Nothing made a rejection sting harder than cold hard silence. We were sitting on his couch and I it was done with the silent treatment. I said, "I'd like to go home now."

I was too exhausted to hold it together and it wouldn't be fair to cry in front of him. Home was the best option.

"Not yet." He dropped his hand down on my thigh as he sat next to me on the sofa and squeezed it gently.

"I want to talk to you," he whispered. He sounded as exhausted as I was.

My shoulders sagged in disappointment but I wasn't surprised. "We can do our last night tomorrow, Eamon. I'm too tired right now."

He turned to me, a frown covering his face. "So you lied?" he said.

I blinked. "Lied? What did I lie about?"

"You said you wanted to be with me an hour ago and now you want to talk about rescheduling our last fuck?"

Oh. That. "Your silence spoke volumes, so if you're looking for me to beg or cry and scream, I'm too tired." And to emotionally scarred.

"I want you to tell me what you want," he said.

I mustered a smile. "I already did. You, Eamon. I want you." I cupped his face again, staring into his eyes. "Just. You."

"Good, because I want you too, Layla. So fucking bad."

He didn't wait for my response before his lips were on mine, devouring my mouth like it was his last meal. He tasted of whiskey or maybe it was scotch, but it was spicy and rich. Strong.

"Layla," he moaned.

He pulled back and stared at me, brushing a thumb over the bruise on my cheekbone and then trailing another finger over the bloodstain on my forehead.

"Eamon, please. Love me."

He flashed a grin that was halfway between boyish and rakish before leaning in for another taste. "I already do."

I wanted more details. I wanted him to say those three words, to hear his sexy timber as he grunted those words in my ear but when his tongue dipped into the hollow of my throat and when his hands cupped my breasts, I was lost.

Totally fucking lost.

"Eamon, please."

My hands roamed over him, hungry to feel every inch of his sculpted body. I wanted to look at him, but I was too desperate to touch him and taste him, to give him the same pleasure he gave to me.

"Yes, Layla, yes."

His hands, his mouth were everywhere, and he tore at my clothes until I was naked. Until his clothes were strewn over mine and the hair on his chest scraped against my own smooth skin.

"It's been too fucking long," he growled in my ear.

I agreed, but my throat wouldn't work, not when his mouth took a nipple, licking and sucking it until I moaned out loud. He moved back and forth on my breasts, making me feel like my body and brain had been disconnected and the only thing I could do was feel.

"Too long," he kept saying over and over.

We came together and it was fast and rough, inelegant but oh so incredible. His mouth worked magic on every inch of my skin, electrifying me everywhere he touched. It was amazing, a feeling I'd never experienced as he pumped into me. Slow and deep and hard, his gaze never left mine and every push brought us closer together. Closer to the knife's edge of pleasure.

"Layla. Oh, Layla."

My name came out on a low growl as one hand cupped my thigh and his deep strokes came faster. Harder.

"Eamon, I'm. So. Close."

His smile was predatory and his gaze dark like a man on a mission. "I love watching you come, Layla and I love the way you clench around me. Hell, I just fucking love you baby."

And dammit if that didn't push me right over the edge into a shattering orgasm that was more like an out of body experience. If not for the look in Eamon's eyes as he thrust, then froze and shook as his own orgasm roared through his body, I might have thought I was dreaming. Or worse, dead. But the benefit of an outer body experience was getting to see that look of love shining in his eyes even as pleasure coursed through him.

Eamon collapsed on top of me and the weight of his big, warm, ultra-masculine body was enough to send another round of shockwaves bouncing through me.

"Oh, Layla."

"Say it again," I urged him because I needed to hear it again and I needed to know those words weren't spoken in lust.

He pulled back with a smile. "I am in love with you, Layla."

My heart stuttered to a stop before it kicked into overdrive and tried to beat its way out of my chest. "That's good because I am so in love with you too. You saved me," I told him quietly as tears trekked down my face.

"I'll always save you. Always protect you."

"Always?"

"And then some, babe."

Suddenly the night—or the morning—didn't seem so bad.

Epilogue

Layla ~ One month later

I gestured for Eamon, sitting next to me on the couch, to give me a moment to wrap up the phone call with my dad. He curled his arm around my shoulder and kissed my temple by way of an answer. A month had passed since my kidnapping, but Dad still wasn't convinced that I'd made the right decision by sticking with Eamon. Hell, I wasn't convinced, but the way he held me, the way he looked into my eyes, I couldn't fathom being without him.

"And you're sure his family is going to protect you?"

"Yes, Dad. I told you, there are guys protecting me around the clock and Eamon's house is pretty much a fortress. There are guys protecting you as well."

He paused. "I was wondering about that. Ever since I started going to rehab, I've seen the same car drive up and down my street."

"Well now you know."

Eamon's cell phone rang. He unwound himself from me, stood up from the couch and crossed to the other side of the room to answer it. I turned my attention back to my conversation.

"Look, Dad, I know this all started in a strange and ugly way, but please believe me when I say I'm happy. Eamon treats me like a princess and even though he's rough around the edges, he really is a big ole teddy bear."

Eamon gave me a wink when he heard that. I grinned back at him, hearing at the same time Dad's deep sigh travel through the phone line.

"Okay, sweetheart," he said. "Just, please be careful. You know what that man can do."

"I will, Dad. I love you."

"I love you too. Call me tomorrow."

I smiled. "Sure thing, Dad. Bye."

I slid the phone onto the coffee table. Eamon had finished his call and returned to the couch. He slid next to me and curled his arm around my waist and I cupped his cheek with my hand and pulled him close to me.

If last month was crazy as hell, this month had been heaven on earth. Eamon had been more than I could have ever hoped in a man. Sweet and attentive, still bossy and sexy as hell, and every day he told me how much he loved me.

Yeah, my life didn't suck anymore.

"What's that grin for?" he asked.

I was staring at me with an affectionate smile on his lips. "I was just thinking about my hot boyfriend who spoils me rotten."

Eamon rolled his eyes, wrapping me in his arms and pulling me onto his lap.

"I want to spoil you woman, but you make it damn hard."

It was true. He'd tried to buy me jewelry and clothes and even a car over the past week, but I didn't want any of it.

"With the way you look at me, I have everything I need."

"Believe me I get plenty out of looking at you." He smacked a kiss on my neck and squeezed tight. "I'm going to spoil you the rest of your life. Just wait."

Who would've ever thought the asshole mobster I found pounding my dad's face in with his fists would end up the love of my life? Certainly not me, and certainly not my dad. It turned out Eamon wasn't just a badass enforcer and heir apparent to the Connelly family criminal organization. He was also a romantic.

"You already do spoil me. Clearing my dad's debt was more than enough."

Eamon offered to pay for rehab for Dad, and at first, we didn't think he was ready, but finally Dad accepted the help and was in outpatient groups every day. "I appreciate all that you want to do, Eamon, but you're all that I need."

"You know that only makes me love you more, right?"

I did know and it told me a lot about the man I'd fallen for and his trust issues.

"All part of my evil plan to get you to fall so in love with me you never fall out."

"Not gonna be a problem, princess. You're stuck with me. And the family."

That part still took some getting used to, but his family was great, at least the three I'd met so far. Rourke was the quiet one, Shae was the charming one and Patrick was the father. The leader. The head of the Connelly family. They were all handsome men who carried themselves with the kind of confidence that came from knowing your place in the world. It was hard to remember they were ruthless gangsters when I watched them razz each other over video games or fight over the last piece of meat.

"No place I'd rather be."

"Good because we have some unfinished business." His smile turned sensual and his touch softened.

"Do we?"

His smile turned serious and his eyes softened. "We do. I love you Layla and I want to make sure you're mine, that I can protect you, love you, for the rest of our lives."

He reached into his pocket and pulled out a deep blue box and flipped the lid open.

My hands flew to my face and I shrieked, "Oh my God!"

It was a gigantic sapphire in a princess cut setting with what seemed like thousands of diamonds circling it like icy ballerinas. I could barely breathe I was so surprised.

"It's gorgeous, Eamon."

"Not as gorgeous as you," he grinned, but with nervous tremor in his voice.

"Layla Julene Michaels, will you marry me?"

Tears pooled in my eyes and I shook my head eagerly. He took the ring out of the box and slipped it on my finger. I wrapped my arms around him, trapping the ring box between us as I dotted his face with kisses.

"I can't wait to marry you, Eamon." I pulled back with a frown. "You don't think it's too soon?"

"Fuck no," he said gruffly. "I'd marry you tonight if you'd go for it."

I could see the hope written all over his face and I nearly agreed on the spot.

"Tonight is a little soon," I said, my head spinning and my heart overflowing with love. "But I hear spring weddings are nice."

Springtime in Rocket was gorgeous, and it would make for a memorable wedding day.

Eamon's face darkened and I worried he had changed his mind.

"Spring is months away," he grumbled. "It's too long."

"There is one way I might marry you sooner," I told him playfully.

"What is it?" His gaze was serious. Dark.

"Let's have a baby."

He growled and nibbled my ear, using his weight to lay me back on the sofa. "I'm going to give you all the babies you want."

Those were the words I wanted to hear. My legs circled his waist and crossed at the ankles. "Eamon? Can we start now?"

"Yes. Damn, I love to hear you moan my name," he all but roared, sliding his denim covered cock back and forth between my thighs.

"I love when you make me moan your name."

"I live for it," he said in a tone that stole my breath away. I pulled him down for a forceful kiss that set my body on fire.

My shirt was on the floor and one hand was down his pants when his phone vibrated on the coffee table beside us. "You've got to be kidding me."

"Nope." Eamon reached for the phone but his gaze never left mine. His hips pushed forward, adding a torturous amount of pleasure to the wet spot between my legs.

"Yeah?"

As I watched Eamon, his smile quickly faded, and then turned serious. "Everything okay," I mouthed but he nodded and brushed me off.

A short pause then just as he hung up the phone he said, "Those Milano motherfuckers."

The Milano name filled me with no small amount of fear. The last time I heard that name, I was tied to a chair by a fat, stinking ginger. "What do they want? Revenge?"

Eamon let out a long sigh and rubbed his forehead. "Doubtful. They aren't leaving Reno. I think this is less about revenge and more about a hostile fucking takeover. Those sorry motherfuckers want the family's business, but the Connelly's don't bend over for anyone."

I swallowed against the lump in my throat and leaned into Eamon. I knew I'd told my dad that we were protected, safe. And I truly believed we were. But I couldn't shake the feeling that things were about to get a helluva lot worse.

I turned to Eamon and held his face in my hands. "Go after these fuckers, babe. Do what you have to but please, come back to me."

His expression melted and a smile crossed his beautiful face. "Always. Babe. Always."

* * * *

~ THE END ~

Acknowledgements

Thank you so much for making my books a success! I appreciate all of you! Thanks to all of my beta readers, street teamers, ARC readers and Facebook fans. Y'all are THE BEST!

And a huge very special thanks to Jessie! I'm such a *hot mess, but without your keen sense of organization and skills, I'd be a burny fiery inferno of hot mess!! Thank you!

And a very special thanks to my editors (who sometimes have to work all through the night! *See HOT MESS above!) Thank you for making my words make sense.

About The Author

KB Winters is a Wall Street Journal and USA Today Bestselling Author of steamy hot books about Bikers, Billionaires, Bad Boys and Badass Military Men. Just the way you like them. She has an addiction to caffeine, tattoos and hard-bodied alpha males. The men in her books are very sexy, protective and sometimes bossy, her ladies are...well...*bossier*!

Living in sunny Southern California, with her five kids and three fur babies, this embarrassingly hopeless romantic writes every chance she gets!

You can reach me at:

Facebook.com/kbwintersauthor

kbwintersauthor@gmail.com

www.Kbwinters.com

Made in the USA
Lexington, KY
04 June 2019